NIGHT RAID!

Flood made out an island of trees and brush in the sea of grass. Along its length, men were shooting at spaced intervals. "I'd like to see if they wouldn't flush out in the open," he said.

Coe chuckled. "I think they will. Let's try."

Flood's first lunge put his horse deep in the thicket, and Flood heard a gun cease firing and some muted bitter words as a man fought a horse, and they both crashed clear. Flood turned his horse at right angles down the middle, his guns spitting lead.

"Oh damn, damn!" a voice said, and Flood pulled up short. He knew that voice, and would always know it. It was Margot Curtain's. . . !

THE
BRANDED
MAN

Luke Short

A DELL BOOK

CHAPTER ONE

IN THE COURSE of an improbable five minutes what had been a difference in opinion had changed to an argument to what was now a near violent quarrel. Mark Flood was the first to see its threat and he reached for the pipe in his shirt pocket, avoiding old Jim Wheat's angry gaze. For perhaps thirty seconds of dead silence in which Mark packed his pipe and held his reins pressed in the crook of his elbow to his side, he marshaled his rights in his own mind.

They were slim enough, and apt to be slimmer. But they were rights, unalterable as only the rights of a trail boss can be. He folded his arms, intending to lean on the saddle-horn, but his horse, forefeet half down the sloping river bank, needed only the forward shift of his weight in the saddle to step down beside Wheat's horse already standing in a foot of water and quartering the bank. Instead, Mark stretched his legs in the stirrups, took reins in hand, and removed the pipe from his mouth.

"I have said all I will, Jim. This isn't a fit thing."

"No," Wheat agreed curtly, and his voice had lost none of the phlegmy thickness of an old man's anger. "Still, when you say this bottom would bog a saddle blanket, I mean to prove you are wrong. Look at my horse. He's been standing in it these five minutes."

Mark said nothing, but his eyes were dark with impatience.

"Mind, I like caution, especially in the young," Wheat went on. "But Shifflin is already two days ahead of us in a strange country with three thousand head of our cattle." He gestured with a thick slow hand across the wide river toward the west, where the far blue-black mountains continued to shoulder into a tangle of storm clouds as they had done all day.

"We wait for those rains to reach here and we'll be water-bound another day, maybe two." His hand dropped. "We've got two hours of daylight yet, time enough and to spare to drive our herd across. I mean to do it."

Mark gauged the determination in Wheat's voice, and found it bluff. He wheeled his horse up the bank, then said flatly, "If you or any man with stuff in that herd wants to try it—even with his own stuff, mind— then you'll have to vote a new trail boss. If you don't, then tell Ringgold to throw the herd over on that feeder creek for water and bed them down."

His voice was unequivocal as he finished, as if he had put away patience and tolerance for authority, which he had. The faint distant rumble of the approaching trail herd to the south came and died through the shore cottonwoods, and he added, "I'd like it done quick."

Wheat yanked viciously at his reins and walked his horse up the bank and past Flood, saying grimly, "Maybe we've waited too long for that vote."

Flood said nothing, watching the broad expanse of shirt back Wheat presented before he threaded the trees and lifted his pony into a lope.

Mark sat his pony solidly, unmoving, clenching his pipe comfortably in his teeth, and thinking how bad fortune seems to breed bad fortune. He was not thinking of Wheat and his stubborn determination to drive the trail herd across the Ruidoso here before dark. At least three of the men back there with the cattle could tell Wheat that a bottom that will cross a horse or even a remuda will bog down heavy lead steers in short order, especially when high water, such as was certainly here last night, had come and gone and left the subsurface sand still sogged.

No, it wasn't that. Rather, Flood was thinking of what he had seen on the bedground across the river and of what Wheat hadn't seen when, less than an hour ago, they had scouted ahead of their herd to the river here, expecting to find the three thousand head of cattle held by Shifflin and his ten men waiting to join herds.

Neither Shifflin nor his men nor the cattle were there. Wheat and Flood had made a cursory survey of the bedground, making sure Shifflin had already been here, and it was then that Wheat had attempted to force Flood to unwise decision. Wheat was sure Shifflin had drifted his herd north, after tiring of waiting.

But Flood, recalling what he had seen and kept from Wheat, was not so sure of this. He looked back now and Wheat was out of sight. There had come a soberness into Flood's squarish weather-browned face now that Wheat was gone and even the straight, flat way he sat the saddle was different. His wide shoulders were hunkered down a little, as if with weariness, and he carried his hat now as he sloped his horse down the bank and forded the river.

On the far bank he reined over to the right and made for a thicket of small cottonwoods thrust far back from the bank, moving with the certainty of a man who knows what he is looking for. By the thicket, he pulled up and dismounted.

There, as he expected, he found the sodden ashes of Shifflin's fire close to the thicket. Erect, Flood was not an overly tall man, but he had an economy, almost an indolence, of movement that men tall and sure of themselves seem to possess; so that now, walking slowly, apparently aimlessly, glance on the ground, he seemed lost in idle reflection.

The set of the gray eyes deep in his skull and sleepy slow beneath heavy eyebrows, the same color as his thick, crisp chestnut hair, furthered this impression. So did his clothes, which were careless and worn waist overalls and gray flannel shirt. But the high heels of his scuffed and rag-soft half boots were not run over, and the shell belt with pendent holster slantwise across his flat hips was dark with oil, so that to the observant he might have been catalogued as a man of contradictions, indolent yet aware, careless of trifles, cautious of essentials. If this need more proving, there was the gun at his hip, the steel of it worn bright, but the butt unchipped and the visible screw-heads scarred with tightening.

His mouth now was pursed a little, and his eyes had come awake, searching. He was thinking, fumbling, guessing and with ponderous unhaste was trying to build a mental picture of what had passed here. He reasoned that since it was raining the night Shifflin was here, the chuck wagon would have been pulled almost under the trees, and the men would have thrown their bedrolls at the edge of this thicket.

That much was clear, so he walked over to its edge. Slowly, half-stooping now, he skirted the boundary of this brush. Five times he knelt and picked up .45 caliber six-gun shell cases. When they became so numerous he could see them without kneeling, he dropped those in his hand and stood still, looking at the ground, then at the brush, then at the ground again.

These were what he had seen and not mentioned to Wheat. And now, contemplating the number of them, he knew there had been a fight here, a hard fight.

Thoughtfully, he walked to the nearest cottonwood and squatted against it, lighting his pipe.

At first, thinking, he dismissed these discoveries of the last hour and pieced together what he knew of this. Two hundred miles back on the trail, their herd of six thousand cattle had been split, because, for men unused to the tricks of trail driving, it had proved too big and unwieldy. Hank Shifflin, as the only man besides Flood familiar with the tasks of the trail drive, had been elected trail boss, given ten men and sent ahead with three thousand cattle, half the herd. He was to proceed at his discretion until he reached the Ruidoso River where the trail turned east and followed the river until both crossed the American and Chisholm Trails. Rains and stampedes had put Flood with the remaining three thousand cattle almost three days behind Shifflin.

It had been decided by these dozen ranchers and their hands who had pooled their herds for this drive that when they reached the Ruidoso River at this point, they would join the herds again, cross the river, flank the Rockies across country and pick up far to the north the trail that led to the mining camps, the destination their beef contract called for. This, instead of making a wide detour to the east over the Chisholm Trail with its unnecessary detour of hundreds of miles.

All this was reasonable, Flood thought, yet it ceased being so right here. Shifflin had been here. He was gone now, with two hats full of shell cases to attest his passing.

Flood sucked steadily at his pipe, dreading the conclusion he must make. He knew without even saying it to himself that it had been his responsibility. He had conceived the idea, had journeyed north last winter to the Colorado mining camps to make the contract, and had lifted this little band of small ranchers out of the dreary rut of their existence. By his work and judgment, he had already brought them and their fortunes three hundred miles up the trail—to what?

Again he looked over the bedground and noted without any interest that the western sky was blacker and a ground breeze that was riding off the hills was sullen to his face.

He rose and put on his hat and said aloud, "But a herd that size doesn't disappear." Yet he was thinking only of the men. Ten men and Shifflin, vanished with three thousand head of cattle.

Swinging up on his pony, he determined to spend the time until dark in what he knew would be a fruitless effort to pick up the trail of the vanished herd. He and Wheat had circled this bedground once, and, in the face of the fact that there had been three rains in as many days, Wheat had given up search for tracks, saying that Shifflin had moved north. Flood knew better.

He struck off across the small basin that tilted to the north, crossed that ridge in high grass, and sloped down to a rolling plateau. Immediately, perhaps a mile to the north, he saw a wagon, and after a moment's watching, recognized it as the chuck wagon of Shifflin's herd. It was solitary, pulled by four mules being driven at an unwise speed.

Flood angled off to it and in another moment it changed course for him. They met in the rising wind by a bare dune, and Flood saw fat Casey Cummins, the cook, lean back and drop the ribbons and slide over in the seat to his side.

"Where's Shifflin, Mark? Did he turn back?"

Flood was already shaking his head, when Casey asked, "Then where is he?"

"You've been north?" Flood asked.

"A day and a half, following a trail that petered out in the hills. I cut back east again, thinking I'd missed him."

"Where were you?"

"Cibola Ford over east, getting grub," Cummins said. He was looking at Flood's face and Flood looked away.

"He didn't turn back?" Casey asked again, slower.

"No. Did you leave the herd bedded down yonder to wait for us?"

Cummins nodded.

"Then he's gone," Flood said gently. "The men and cattle. Not a sign. There are a dozen trails of cattle a man can follow—all going west for the hills."

"What happened?"

"Man, don't you know? I found more than a hundred empties where the fire lay."

Neither of them spoke for a moment, then Cummins laughed uneasily and shook his head. "It don't happen that way, Mark." And when Flood said nothing, Cummins said softly, "God."

"There's no heavy trail going north?" Mark asked again, in quiet desperation.

"No."

Mark said wearily, "Come along, Casey."

CHAPTER TWO

ON THE WAY BACK, Cummins asked questions and Flood answered him absently, laconically, until the cook fell silent too.

They found the herd being bedded for the night on a strip of clear prairie bordering a feeder stream. At the

sight of the four riders circling the vast herd in the dusk,
Flood's face did not change, even though he knew he
had won his argument with Wheat. But only this argument, for the one he felt sure would come was not yet
won. Thinking thus, he ran his third finger along his
shell belt, knowing it was full and heavy, yet wanting
to feel the shells just the same. He avoided touching the
gun at his hip, and instead pointed, and said, "Make a
wide circle, Casey. They're uneasy tonight under that
sky."

Flood's chuck wagon was pulled up beside the stream,
and a fire was going. The rope corral was already set up
by the wagon, the remuda corralled, the men slinging
the bedrolls from the wagon, rustling wood and putting
the camp in order.

The approach of the Shifflin chuck wagon brought
the camp to a standstill, then there were shouted greet-
ings which Cummins barely answered. Flood rode
straight for the rope corral and gave his horse over to
the wrangler, Lew Wakefield.

"Saddle my gray, will you, Lew?" he asked, as he dismounted.

Lew had the reins and he looked over the pony's neck
at Flood.

"Trouble?"

"Yes," Flood answered, and skirted the corral toward
the fire. As he entered its circle of light, he straightened
up and slowed his walk. The men were gathered about
Cummins, listening, and Flood's gaze singled out those
men he thought were with him. Then he was suddenly
ashamed of this, and cleared his throat and joined the
group.

They split for him, looking at him and at Cummins.

"Is this true, Flood?" Frank Lisbon asked. Flood
glanced at Wheat and then nodded, and said, "I'm
afraid so, Frank," because Lisbon was almost an old
man and a good one.

"Maybe we'd better get this from the first," Flood
said in the silence. Even the cook was listening, rubbing
the flour off on his sacking apron.

"Start from when you left camp, Cummins."

Cummins's red face was harried and sweating and he took off his hat and put it on again before he began. "Like I said, I left Shifflin's camp the morning after we got in. Shifflin thought I could pack back enough grub from Cibola Ford to do us and you too, and it would save you a trip. It took two days. I pulled in here last night in the rain and found the herd moved.

"Shifflin never told me he aimed to move, but I thought he might have grazed ahead. This morning I started north on the trail, going by signs, of course, which wasn't any too plain. They kept angling west, and by noon they had taken to the hills. I knew then it wasn't our herd, so I cut east, feeling sure I'd cut their trail."

He paused and looked at Flood, and Flood nodded. "There's been nothing but range cattle between the hills and the river," Cummins said.

"Are you sure of that, Casey?" Ringgold asked quietly. He stood a head above the other men in physique and ability, a lean man with very pale gray eyes in a long face that was slashed by a full mustache entirely hiding his mouth and almost muffling his voice.

"Yes," Cummins said emphatically. "Three thousand head of cattle would tramp and eat a swath in that tall grass that a man could follow in the dark. Besides leaving signs. No, they're not north, Chris, and I say it knowing there was three heavy rains since I left."

The men looked at each other and at Cummins. The cook went back to the wagon and work, and Ringgold turned and walked over to a bedroll and sat down. The others spread out in a loose half circle around Flood, who sat on a bedroll too.

"That don't happen," Ringgold said slowly, looking to Flood for corroboration. "Three thousand head of heavy beef herded by ten-eleven men don't jump the country that way. Why, without a man riding herd, they'd stick together."

"They didn't, though, Chris," Flood said. "Here's what I found." He told them of finding the fire, and close by, the empty shell cases.

"All right," Lisbon said, when he was finished. "There was a fight, maybe. But that don't account for the men under Shifflin."

"I reckon if you'll look over these hills close, it will, Frank," Flood replied.

No one said anything for a moment and then Hank Teacher, a young rancher and Flood's closest neighbor at home, said, "You mean they've been killed."

"That's what I think."

When they just looked at him, he ripped up a handful of grass and kneaded it between his two fingers while he talked. "Those hills to the west are close, and behind them are mountains and a country we don't know, except that it keeps piling up into the Rockies to the north. Suppose we were fifteen men who wanted to steal a herd of cattle. Remember, the night Shifflin got in it was raining. After the cattle were bedded down, six of Shifflin's men would be riding herd to quiet the cattle. The rest would be trying to sleep or be drying out by the fire at the chuck wagon. If we wanted to steal the herd, we'd have to kill Shifflin and all his men. All right. Eight of our men on a dark, rainy night could take care of the herders. The other seven, coming along the river bank, would have the noise of the rain and the river to cover their coming. When the first shot cracked, our men could ride into camp." He spread his hands gently. "Every man would be killed. The cattle would stampede to the west away from the noise, run against those steep hills and fan out. A crew of fifteen men could have them rounded up by morning. The big herd would be split into small herds of two hundred or so, and could be driven into the hills at a dozen different places."

"But the men," Ringgold said. "Where are their bodies?"

"Buried somewhere back in these hills. Two men working an hour could carry them back and cave a cutbank in on them. Not even the buzzards would bother them then."

When Ringgold said nothing, Flood went on. "Remember, there have been three rains since that night. They would take care of all the signs."

The men watched him long after he had finished speaking, and then Lisbon said, "Why do you think all this, Flood?"

"Because I saw two distinct trails going into those hills to the west, Frank, trails of small herds. They're faint, but plain enough. Cummins followed another trail in."

Wheat had been watching Flood up till now, and he took his gaze from Flood and looked at Ringgold.

"I've heard tell of that," he said softly, as if he were trying to remember it all. "Didn't a steal like that happen on this same trail last year sometime, so folks tell?"

The attention switched to Wheat, and Flood did not move, but his pulse quickened.

"From what I heard tell, it didn't happen far from here," Wheat continued. "Back maybe fifty miles."

He looked fleetingly at Flood, and then over at Teacher, who had said, "I never heard it, but then I wouldn't. Did it go like this?"

"Not exactly," Wheat said, frowning. His broad and seamed face had lost some of its flush, and his voice was muted, as any good storyteller's is. Flood, though he didn't see it, could imagine the dreamy maliciousness in Wheat's faded eyes. Wheat stuck a straw in his mouth and talked around it to all the men except Flood, whom he ignored.

"Seems like a trail cutter stopped a big Munro herd down by these Point Loma breaks. He had papers and such from the neighboring ranchers authorizing him to cut out the local range cattle that had strayed into the Munro trail herd. Naturally, that stopped the herd, and when the cutting began, it bunched the Munro hands pretty much. That was just the way they were when a gang of riders poured down out of the breaks. They shot up the Munro outfit, killed a few men, and got away with the herd. The trail cutter rode off with them, of course, since he was part of the gang."

"Did Munro get back any of his stuff?" Teacher asked.

Wheat shook his head. "Not a head. His trail boss and what men were left rode after the herd, but the rustlers stopped to fight. The Munro outfit did get the trail cutter, though. Seems like he was the leader of the gang." He looked up at Flood, whose face was shadowed in the light of the fire the cook had let die.

"I knew his name, once—this trail cutter," Wheat said. He spoke to Flood now. "He was hanged right there, wasn't he, Flood?"

Flood nodded.

"Remember his name, Flood?"

Again Flood nodded. "It was my brother, Gordon Flood," he said in a voice without inflection.

"That was it," Wheat said, rising carelessly, as Flood's quiet voice ripped the silence.

"You're not done, Wheat. Go on."

Wheat turned to him and said with no guile in his voice now, "No, Flood, I'm not. It was hard lines I had to be sitting on your corral poles when that gunman rode up and tried to blackmail you to keep this about your brother quiet among us, your friends. And I admired you when you beat him up and sent him on his way. Even though you didn't ask me to, Flood, I've kept that quiet."

"Something I never asked for, Wheat, but I liked you for it."

Wheat's speech now was as thick as it had been in the afternoon. He took a step out closer to the fire, and there was the hard, rugged dignity of a fighter in his face and in the set of his wide old shoulders. Wakefield, who had been standing by the hind wheel of the wagon, sauntered over and sat down cross-legged beside Flood.

"Flood made our contract at the camps last winter," Wheat said, talking now to Lisbon, the only other old head. "He rode this trail and mapped it out. He set the date for the drive. He even"—and here he paused for emphasis—"split the herd and threw us three days behind Shifflin."

Flood stood up now and drew his gun and cocked it

and hefted it pleasantly, his face unsmiling. "I'll finish it, Wheat," he said gently, tolerantly. He looked over the men, who did not rise nor move, while Wakefield sat calmly beside him. The cook behind him cleared his throat and stood still.

"What you're getting at is that I planned this steal with these friends of my brothers, then split the herd so it would be possible." He smiled and there was no mirth in it. "Would you say I made it rain, too, Wheat, so their getaway could be made easier?"

Wheat said doggedly, "I don't have to say much, Flood. That gun finished it."

"Wheat, sit down and shut up!" Ringgold whipped out. Wheat did not move, although his right wrist was touching the butt of his gun.

Ringgold then said, "Flood, put that gun up."

"He won't shoot," Wheat said.

"That's right," Flood said, watching Wheat in the flicker of the dying fire. "A fool lives long, Wheat, providing he runs with honest men." To Ringgold, he said, "I pulled this gun because Wheat would have done it in a moment, Chris."

"I know that."

"What I've got to say is short," Flood said, looking around the circle. "You men have got your fortunes tied up in that bedground out there. Is there a one of you that will leave his and come with me?"

"Where?" Gilroy, a pleasant-faced man of fifty, asked after a moment's pause.

"I don't know. I'm going to find where Shifflin's herd is and if he and his men are dead. I'm going to find our cattle."

When no one spoke, he said, "I'm not blaming you. A man's misfortune is strictly his own, but I wanted to ask."

"I'll go," Ringgold said.

"Not you, Chris. You're needed to pull this outfit through."

"I will," Wakefield said.

"Nor you. You're in debt to Wheat now, Lew. Nor

you, Cummins, nor you, cook. Is there anyone else?"

Nobody spoke and Flood said to Wakefield, "Is my gray saddled?"

"Ground-haltered by Cummins's wagon."

"Then don't follow me," Flood said. "Chris, in your place I'd cut over to the American and take a chance on selling the stuff at Dodge. Bank my share there, and get rid of my remuda for what it will bring and bank it too. And now, Lew, when you've got a pair of double blankets, a can of coffee, some matches and a lard bucket on my rig, I'll go."

Lew went over to the chuck wagon, and Flood stood straight and silent, his face in alert repose. He only spoke once and that was to Wheat.

"Wheat, Ringgold is the best head. Make him trail boss."

Wheat only said, "You're gone, Flood, but you'll never ride long or hard enough to shake eleven dead men."

"I'm sorry you believe that," Flood said.

"All right, Mark," Wakefield said.

Flood backed out of the circle of firelight to the side of his gray. "Thanks, Lew. So long," he said swiftly, as he holstered his gun and mounted. In a second, he was clear.

A shot slogged the thick night air, but Flood didn't hear the sing of the slug.

He looked back and saw a moil of struggling men in the dim firelight.

"A stubborn man," he said of Wheat, and then turned his horse toward the river.

CHAPTER THREE

ON THE THIRD NOON after he left the Ruidoso, and a half day after all signs of the split herd had disappeared, Flood admitted defeat. The first day he had taken the trail of the herd Cummins had followed and trailed it through miles of breaks whose canyon-cut shale and rock hills lifted hourly to the great barrier rim in the west. Here the side of a great mesa rose whose level rim curved north and south to seeming infinity, and whose slough of ages formed all the foothills he had passed through. Atop it was grassland and timber, a rolling, tilting range of green that climbed to the great staggered peaks of the mountains which walled out the west with rock and the snows of centuries.

And from the rim, where Flood stopped to blow his horse and look about him, he could see this was grazed range, and that the trail herd could be swallowed up in the anonymity of these herds and in the vastness of the country.

But he wanted to be sure of this much, and he rode the rim for a day to the south. By that evening, he noted the places where ten small herds had climbed to the rim and vanished toward the west, and he was fairly certain of two more. That evening he paused just before the mesa threw the great cape of its shadow over the breaks below, and he was more sure now that Shifflin and his ten men were buried somewhere down there, buried during rain, and their graves covered by rain.

On this morning, he had taken the faint tracks of one herd, which led toward the heart of the range. In an hour he had lost them among a tangle of used cattle trails which bore hundreds of tracks fresher than those he wanted. Here, by a stream, where cattle had watered this morning, he dismounted, stretched, filled his pipe and considered. His prediction made to the assembled men at Ruidoso had been pretty accurate. The big herd had been split into a dozen small ones for mobility, had been driven up and across this barrier rim and were now on this range, scattered as leaves, no doubt. Then he must go on. He would be a stranger in this land, whose horse fortunately did not bear the Triangle Dot road brand of the trail herd and its remudas. Nothing about him differed from a casual rider of the chuck line. He bore a name that would get him quickly killed or as quickly befriended, if this was, as he supposed, the country of men who had stolen the Munro herd and Shifflin's herd.

So he rode on, and by mid-afternoon had picked up a wagon trail that angled a little south and west and finally tilted down to a deep valley, where lay a town.

He kept to the lowering road and crossed the bridge over a full stream, turned sharply left and was in the town. Like a thousand of its sisters, it sprawled along a wide main street always fetlock deep in either dust or mud. Its false-front clapboard buildings were uniformly angular and unpainted, yet by small signs such as the size of the hotel and feed stable and by the amount and condition of the glass in its store windows, it betrayed its prosperity. Flood noted this, and leisurely, as a man will, set about trying to discover the name of the town without having to ask. By comparing signs on stores, he found that two of them carried the name Clearcreek —written as one word—in connection with the announcement of business.

Musing on this, trying to recall the name, he noted another thing, and his mind was yanked to instant awareness. Ahead of him were the bigger buildings. The hitch-rack on the right side of the street was empty, except for one somnolent and hip-shot pony tied there. To the hitch-rack on the left side were tied two groups of a dozen or so horses each, with perhaps a hundred feet of free rail between them. In front of each group of horses, there was a clot of men on the sidewalk in compact, watchful attention. Midway between these two was a saloon, proclaimed so by the weathered strip of sign above the door bearing the legend *Palace Saloon*.

As Flood rode by, the men in the nearest group fell silent, and watched him pass. His level stare was returned, and returned again by the second group, and then he swung into the feed stable beyond and dismounted, giving his gray over to a crippled old man with instructions to grain it. It occurred to him as he looked across the street from the wide stable door that perhaps he was expected, and then he dismissed this and angled across the street to the hotel. He knew without looking that these men were still watching him, and he wondered what it was in the saloon that they were awaiting or guarding.

He was stopped in mid-street by the voice of the stableman calling, "This horse is lamed, mister."

Flood stopped and turned, and said, "That's an old stone bruise that bothers him on rock."

The stableman nodded and Flood looked at the nearest group of men, who had been listening and were still watching him. He flushed a little when he turned, thinking he was a fool to have said it publicly, that he could have ridden in from only one direction and that the east. But on the far walk he wondered why not, because he was riding the chuck line with a footsore horse, and the east was as good a direction as any to come from.

The hotel was old and big, its lobby filled with an orderly clutter of miscellaneous chairs that stretched back to the curving desk in a back corner by the stairs. A girl was seated at the lone writing desk, a man beside her, and she did not even look up from her writing as Flood crossed the lobby to the desk. The man, however, rose and came behind the counter. He was a young man, dressed in an unpressed black suit, and there was a kind of handsome sullenness about his mouth that his dark eyes immediately canceled. They were wide and frank and friendly, but not the eyes of an outdoor man. He said, "Yes, sir?"

"I want a room for a week."

The man turned and after scanning the key-rack, took down a key and said, "I'll show you up."

Flood turned and started for the stairs, when the girl said from behind him, "Lee, you didn't—"

Flood turned, and the girl's voice ceased, and then she said to him, "I'm sorry. Lee always forgets to ask the guests to register. Will you?"

"Yes," Flood said.

She rose and went behind the counter. From under it she brought forth a ledger, and Flood watched her, wishing she would speak again. There was a low throatiness in her speech that a woman seldom has, and a kind of warmth and friendliness that upon analysis, which Flood was to make later, was so habitual and natural that it wasn't friendliness at all. She would have spoken to a dog or a horse or her mother in the same tone, but Flood didn't think this yet, while looking at her. He did, however, when she laid the register on the desk and looked at him. It wasn't the indifference in her face, nor the steady eyes which were so like the gray color of his own that he smiled, but her complete oblivion to the fact she was handsome that made Flood study her. Flood would not have called her pretty, nor beautiful, for there is a sameness of feature in all beautiful women that makes an observant man avoid their monotony. It was character in her face, in her small straight nose whose nostrils moved with her breathing, her wide mouth with the upper lip a little the longer, the clean sweep of her jaw line that pointed slightly at the chin carrying a suggestion of a cleft. There was a strand of tawny hair loose on her forehead, which she made no attempt to brush back. Her dress of dark blue was saved from severity by a white collar, which in turn brought out a kind of golden glow in her skin. She was almost tall, and straight, slender yet giving a suggestion of strength.

As Flood took the pen she offered him and wrote his name, he remembered she had a dusting of freckles across the bridge of her nose, and again he smiled down at the register.

"There's one night's charge subtracted if you keep the room a week," she said, turning the register around and looking at Flood's name.

"All right," Flood said. He hesitated, then said, "I don't think I'll go up."

The young man came down the steps at this announcement, and Flood turned away from the counter. The girl looked up from the register, and said, "If you'd like to leave your luggage, we'll take it up—Mr. Flood."

"I might later," Flood answered. "Thank you."

The girl looked down and Flood saw the flush mounting to her cheeks.

"Yes," she said.

He turned toward the door and he was aware that neither of them had spoken or moved till he was on the walk again. It was as if they had looked at each other, then watched him go out. And it was strange, too, how she hesitated in pronouncing his name. Perhaps this was the greeting his name was bound to evoke in this country, and he thought grimly of Gordie, his wild eyes, his reckless laugh, and his more reckless ways.

Flood already had seen the town marshal's office down the street across from the saloon, now he turned to it. If he wanted to stay in this country, live in it, then he must get work, and if riders were being hired anywhere, the marshal should know it.

It was a small office of one room containing an oversize roll-top desk against the far wall. Back to the desk, sitting in a swivel chair, sat a man with a shotgun laid across his knees and this was the first thing Flood saw as he entered. This man was placed so that he could see across the street. It was his lone horse that was tied to one side of the door at the hitch-rack.

On his vest, Flood noticed, was the star of the sheriff's office. His clothes were careless and soiled, a size too large for his medium big body, but it was his face that Flood's gaze settled on. There were twin deep creases at the side of his nose and mouth, and his blue eyes sat back in his skull, and had a look of quiet curiosity that was not offensive. His face was so tanned that it made his untidy shock of iron-gray hair and his thick eyebrows look white.

"I'm looking for the marshal," Flood said.

"You'll find him across the street," the sheriff replied in a mild voice, gesturing loosely, lazily. "He's busy now, I reckon."

"At the saloon?"

The sheriff nodded, and Flood turned. He paused on the doorsill and looked again at the two groups of men on the far walk who had not moved since he rode into town. And between them gaped the black hole of the saloon entrance gashed by the bat-wing doors. The town was so still now in the strong sunlight that he caught the sense of patient and watchful waiting which these men and the sheriff and the town itself had.

"He'll be through soon," the sheriff said mildly.

Flood nodded and started across the street, and at once he could hear the sheriff rise out of the chair. He could see, too, that the men had stopped conversing and were looking at him.

When he swung under the hitch-rack on to the board-walk, somebody from the group near the stable said, "I wouldn't go in there, mister."

Flood stopped and turned slowly. He tried to find the speaker among the impassive, rough faces that confronted him, and he could not.

"Why?" he asked.

"I wouldn't, that's all," one of the men leaning against the saloon said.

"I'm obliged," Flood said civilly. "Maybe you aren't as thirsty as I am."

CHAPTER FOUR

DELIBERATELY, he shouldered the swing doors aside and stepped into the cool room. For the moment it took to wash the sun-glare out of his eyes, he walked toward the bar on his left, and he was aware that some violent speech had ceased and the sound of his boot heels on the floor filled the silence. The big room with its half dozen card tables was empty except for three men sitting at a table, all of whom stared at him. He looked at them and then said to the bartender who was leaning, arms folded, against the back bar, "Whisky."

The sweat beading the bartender's forehead showed plainly as he looked at the three men. Flood looked too, and the biggest of the three, a slack, flabby man with the worried lines of a hound dog in his face, nodded. This man wore a marshal's badge on his open vest.

"Yes, sir," the bartender said, and his voice was so subdued he cleared his throat in protest.

Flood looked in the bar mirror and saw the table reflected. The three of them were regarding each other in stubborn, walled silence. They wore no guns, Flood noted, and then remembered that every man outside had been armed.

The man Flood could see most clearly was facing the front of the room. He was a big man, barrel-chested, thickset, with a ruddy face whose tight-knit features— blue eyes close together, blunt stub nose, small thin-lipped mouth—made his head seem large and his face at once stupid and crafty below the clean wing of dark hair. He wore clean range clothes, vest over the blue shirt, and his right hand lay on the table fisted on the brim of his hat, his left arm thrown over the chair back. Flood could tell he was at ease, with his mind made up.

The third man had his back to the door, but Flood saw in it the lines of youth. It was straight, tensed, hunched a little because this man had his arms folded on the table. A shock of very light hair tapered to the weather-brown of the neck. He could catch the sharp angle of this man's jaw too.

The sad marshal made a beginning gesture of resuming the conversation, then the rumble in his throat died. He set both blunt fists on the table.

"Like I said, the government threw open this Bear-paw range, so you two would forget this trouble. Its lease is a tenth of what other men would pay, thanks to me and Mayhew. Divide it between you. String an eight-wire fence across it if you want."

"No," the younger man said immediately, flatly. "I couldn't fatten a herd up there on the Bearpaw be-tween snow dates, Honeywell. Besides, that's not the point."

"Uh-huh," the marshal said, looking at the thickset man now. "And you, Hand?"

But the thickset man was already talking in a level,

ponderous voice.

"No. Not the point," he took up. "Maybe you can fob off that snow-pile on Petrie, Sam. It seems you can't. I'm satisfied with a lower range, the Silver Creek, the one I've paid money to use and the one I'll keep. The government can save that Bearpaw range for another time. As far as I know, the Silver Creek range is mine, and it suits me so well I'll fight for it."

"You'll have to," Petrie, the younger man, said quickly.

The marshal heaved his bulk out of the chair and put his weight on his hands which remained on the table top.

"Then be damned to you both," he said with slow heat. "I'll put in my chips now." He looked at one, then the other. "You bring your dog fight into this town and you will need to throw in together to stay in this country. That's very simple and not hard to remember."

He picked up his black hat from the table and started toward the door, then turned, and said, "If you'll take the trouble to step across the street and consult Mayhew, you'll find that goes for the county too."

Hand shoved his chair back and said to the marshal, "All right, Sam. It won't be the first time I have bucked you and won. Mayhew too." He looked at Petrie with calm belligerence and then at the marshal again. "But I say it is queer that a man like you can watch a quiet steal and then be surprised at the violence it breeds. Tell Mayhew that."

Honeywell acted with an agility surprising for his bulk. He leaped toward Petrie and brought both thick hands down on his shoulders, so that Petrie, already half risen out of his chair, was smashed down again. Honeywell held him there and said over his shoulder, "That's enough, Hand. Clear out."

Hand rose, skirted the table and, without looking at either of them, walked past Flood and out the door, where he turned to his right.

Honeywell withdrew his hands and Petrie rose. Flood could see his face now, and it was ugly with anger. It

was a narrow, lean face, arrogant with youth, and the
sultry dark eyes were not deep-set. The throat muscles
were corded, and Flood saw it was an effort for him to
avoid physical violence now. His body seemed not quite
to fit the lean face, for it was solid, big, long muscled,
with broad hulking shoulders that capped the deep
chest, making him seem less tall than he was. He had
broad hands, long fingers that clenched into a square
fist as he looked at the door.

"I won't forget that, Honeywell," he said.

"No," the marshal agreed. "You would rather let
Hand break you in two than make a fool of you. So
would I."

Petrie stood there a moment; and then he relaxed, his
expression clearing into a frown. The marshal cut in
behind him and said to the bartender, "My belt,
George."

When he was handed his gun belt, he strapped it on
deftly and stepped up beside Petrie who was walking
toward the door.

"But don't let it make a bigger fool of you than you
are already, Loosh."

Petrie did not even answer, but shouldered the doors
aside and turned to the left. Honeywell followed him
through and stopped, and as the doors swung to and
flapped and finally died, Flood could see his thick legs
widespread on the sidewalk and the crown of his black
hat turning as he looked up the street and then down
and then up again.

Flood took a sip of his whisky and watched the bartender pour himself a drink and down it, then lean
against the back bar and close his eyes while he ran a
soft, quarter-clenched hand over his face.

When Flood looked out the door again, Honeywell
was gone. He paid for his drink and left. On the street
again, he noticed most of the horses in each group were
still there and a few men were mingling together on
the sidewalk.

Across the street Honeywell slouched in the door of
his office, occasionally turning his head to talk to the

sheriff within.

Flood crossed to him. "You're the marshal?"

Honeywell nodded. "Come in." He turned and Flood followed him into the little room, where again the sheriff nodded to him from the same seat in the same position. Honeywell waved to a chair, and when Flood declined, he leaned against the desk.

"I'm looking for work," Flood began. "Are there outfits around here that would take on a rider?"

"Wasn't you over at the saloon just now?" the marshal asked.

Flood nodded.

"Either of them will take you and pay you fighting wages. I'll pay you ten more a month to stay here with me."

"Thanks," Flood said, smiling slightly. "I don't think I want it."

"No," Honeywell said reflectively, pursing his thick lips, his eyes shrewdly understanding. "It's worth more than ten dollars plus to have twice as many men shooting at you. I can see that, but that is as high as I can go."

"It's not that either," Flood said. "I have got in enough fights trying to keep out of them."

"That's true," the sheriff mused, not looking at Flood. "I've heard gunmen complain of that too."

Flood's gaze whipped to him, but the sheriff was looking out the door to the street.

Honeywell had been shaking his head, and now he spoke. "If I was giving advice that no one asked for, I'd say the thing for a man like you to do is ride."

"Where?"

"Anywhere, just as long as you ride out of this county."

Flood nodded. "Because two outfits fight over a piece of range, do all men quit ranching?"

The marshal nodded too. "Yes. They will. Unless you've lived in the bottom of a well, you know that too."

"I've heard it said," Flood agreed.

"Always. Whatever rancher runs cattle in this country, he does so by sufferance of the big outfits—here, by sufferance of Petrie or Hand. That is, as long as there is peace. When there is war, he takes sides not only because it is human nature to take sides, but because if he doesn't, he is made to. War needs men, and you can't fight a respectable range war with four men and eight guns—not and win it, anyway," Honeywell finished dryly.

Flood, listening, reached for his pipe and his tobacco. Then he stopped and put them away again so that he was looking in Honeywell's sad eyes and missed the humor in the marshal's statement.

"Then if a man is to fight, who should he fight for?" he asked.

"The law," the sheriff said peacefully, still not looking at Flood.

"I won't do that," Flood said. "No man loves a stranger with a whip in his hand." When neither the sheriff nor the marshal commented on that, Flood went on, "If there is any right in this fight, who does it lie with, Petrie or Hand?"

"You walked past thirty armed men to look at them both. What do you think?" Mayhew asked dryly.

"They were both angry. I wouldn't try to say."

Honeywell grunted and looked at Mayhew. "Up to now, neither have we. What do you think, Max?"

"Hand is my sister's boy, but I don't say he's right."

"No," Honeywell said.

"Petrie is greedy," Mayhew continued. "Hand is vindictive. Petrie is stubborn. Hand loves a fight. This whole country is cocked." He looked up at Flood.

"When you walked across the street into the Palace, I believed it would start. A man of mine, a deputy, rode seven hundred miles to ask authority from the land commissioner to throw open the Bearpaw range south of here for a tenth of the lease money it was worth so that Petrie and Hand would quit rowing over the Silver Creek range. It was a gift to them. Our threat with the commissioner was that if he didn't open that range, the troops would have to bury the dead here. We got it.

For three weeks now, we've sweated to get Hand and Petrie together for a parley. We got that too."

He regarded Flood in silence for a brief moment, then went on: "And then when all the dynamite in the county was held in one cleared room and guarded by a gang of men whose blood could never get hotter, you— an armed man, mind, who could be a strange gunman hired by either outfit to kill their unarmed enemy—you walked in that room after a be-damned-to-you speech. You bought a drink and watched Sam here smother a brawl that would have turned the saloon, the town and the county into a shambles."

He paused here, took his mild, reproving gaze from Flood's face and looked out into the street. "A man with foresight enough to know he wouldn't get killed for that ought to have enough left to bet on the right outfit."

Flood flushed. "I had that coming to me."

"You did," the sheriff said.

Flood was walking to the door when Honeywell's voice checked him. "If I was you, I'd give this crowd time to clear out before I said or did much."

Flood was still smarting under the sheriff's jibe as he stepped out on to the walk. He had been a fool to expect either Mayhew or Honeywell to act as recruiting agents for a range war, and he had deserved their reprimand. But beneath it, he saw that this was their way of serving notice that they would not take sides, and would fight this in every way they could. He knew too, that their advice to ride out of this country was well meant, and that it would be wise to take it, but he had already decided to ignore it.

He packed his pipe and lighted it, musing. Hand seemed a thick, stubborn man with a predatory love of battle and a will of iron. A simple man, really, most of whose acts would be predictable. But Petrie was a different stripe, Flood judged. In that brief moment of watching him in the saloon, Flood had dismissed the man's anger, his speech, and noted only the superb arrogance of his face. Flood reckoned him a man with

imagination, and, therefore, possessed of twice the po-
tential danger of Hand. Perhaps this quality would
never help him in a claw and fang range fight if he
were outnumbered and outfought, but if the odds in
men and guns were even, Petrie would win out. Petrie,
then, was Flood's man.

He would talk with Petrie. He crossed toward the
stable to ask if Petrie's outfit had ridden out of town
yet. The stableman had Flood's gray in a stall, and was
rubbing him down. Approaching, Flood immediately
noticed that his bedroll had been taken from the saddle
and he looked around for it.

"I had a bedroll," he said to the old man, his statement a question.

The old man looked up at him. "Lee Curtin over at
the hotel come for it."

Flood nodded, as if dismissing it. "Has Petrie left
town?"

"I reckon not," the old man said, avoiding his eye.
"He wouldn't leave first. It might look like he aimed
to avoid trouble, and that he never does."

Instead of hunting Petrie, Flood left the stable and
went to the hotel, his curiosity roused. The lobby was
deserted, and he shut the door behind him with no
noise. He remembered his room number was seventeen,
so that he did not have to go to the desk, but instead
climbed the stairs. He moved swiftly and with hardly
any noise.

Room seventeen, he found around an L in the hall.
Turning the corner, he raised on tiptoe, but did not
diminish his pace. The door was ajar. He placed a hand
on the panel and pushed it back, and stepped into the
room.

The girl was standing at the side of the bed, looking
at his blankets, which had been unrolled, and at the
blackened coffee pail and coffee can and unopened box
of cartridges which made up his outfit. Lee Curtin stood
at the end of the bed, arms spread on the footboard,
watching her. Neither of them saw the door swing open.

"If I wanted to do that, I would have left him downstairs to watch," Flood said, without any anger in his voice.

The girl started, and turned. Curtin stepped over in front of her, his attitude protective and a little ridiculous. Flood closed the door and leaned against it.

"Sit down," he invited quietly.

The girl looked around, then sat down on the bed, her hands folded on her lap. Curtin stepped to one side. His jaw was outthrust, his face pale, and he kept fisting and unfisting his hands as if expecting something he could not name.

"Have I something you want?" Flood asked the girl.

"No," she answered sullenly.

"It's my name," Flood said. "When you read it, you asked for my outfit. It was so you could look through it, wasn't it?"

"Yes."

"Look here, Flood," Curtin said angrily. "If you've got anything to say, say it to me. Leave her out of this."

Flood ignored him, did not even look at him.

"Did you find what you expected?" Flood asked her.

"No." She looked up at him now, and he could see the shame and misery in her eyes.

"What was it you wanted?"

She did not answer him. Curtin said, "Don't talk, Margot." He said to Flood, "What are you going to do?"

"Would you like to go?" Flood said to the girl.

"Yes."

He opened the door, saying quietly, jeeringly, "I have a few things in my pockets. If you can spare the time, look through them."

She walked past him and he could see the stubborn set to her jaw, the dark flush of humiliation. Then she went down the hall. He turned to Curtin, "Maybe you'd better go too," he said coldly.

Curtin hesitated, then marched past him, and Flood closed the door again.

So he had come to the right place, he reflected, feeling a pleasant pulsing of excitement within him. All this pointed to one thing, that Gordie, who was hanged for his part in the theft of the Munro herd, was known here, and had been here. Flood could not even guess this girl's reason for searching his outfit, but he could not mistake the hate in her eyes. Had Gordie harmed her, so that she hated all Floods or even the name? Flood didn't know, but he reasoned that if she knew the name, then men here knew the name too; and that meant the thieves of the trail herds worked in this country.

He rolled his blankets tightly and went downstairs. The girl was behind the counter, and she watched him defiantly as he approached, and said, "I'm leaving. Is there any charge for this?"

"No charge," she said, then added without any humility, "I'm sorry about that. If you hadn't surprised us, you would never have been our enemy."

"It's happened to me before," Flood said. "That's not why I'm leaving."

"But it has made you our enemy."

"No," Flood said. "I'm sorry you didn't get what you wanted. Or did you?"

"No," she said softly. "If—but if it's revenge they want, will you tell them Lee was innocent?" She paused and looked him straight in the eyes, and hers did not waver. "It was my idea. Truly it was."

Flood only frowned.

"Will you?" she repeated.

"You have the wrong man," Flood said quietly, puzzled.

"Will you?" she persisted, and there was an urgency and passion in her voice that was partly fear. "You don't have to tell them, except that we are to be watched."

Flood said, "Tell who?"

Her face changed and Flood could see the bitterness in her eyes.

"You won't then?" she said.

Flood did not answer. She turned away from him and put her handkerchief to her mouth and hurried, almost ran, through the door behind the desk that let into the dining-room.

Flood stood utterly still a moment, as a man does who

has been promised the answer to a secret and then denied it. Then he acted; he skirted the desk and went
behind it and through the door. In the dining-room, he
paused long enough to see she was not there and then
he made for the kitchen door.

When he swung it open, a blowzy pleasant-faced
woman seated at a long, tin-topped table looked up at
him over a heap of potatoes she was peeling.

"Where is she?"

"Who?"

"Miss Curtin. Is that her name? Where is she?"

"Margot? I don't know," the woman said, after a
pause. "Why?"

"But she came here," Flood said quickly. "I went into
the dining-room and she wasn't there, so I came here.
Where is she?"

"I don't know," the woman repeated.

"But where could she have gone if she didn't come
here?"

The woman laid down her knife with deliberate conviction. "Young man, you've been around enough cook
shacks to know when I say get out I mean it. Get out!"

Flood made an impatient gesture. "But she had to
come here. Did she leave?"

"Get out!"

Flood stepped into the kitchen and looked around,
and then said, "All right."

He did the same in the dining-room and then picked
up his bedroll and went out to look up and down the
street.

And standing on the sidewalk, he realized suddenly
that the surest way to silence this girl forever was to
act the way he was now. He cursed then, because this
was so.

She had assumed he had a voice among many men.
What men? Those that had run with Gordie? And she
had assumed too, that they would and could harm her.
But who they were and why they would harm her, Flood
did not know. His impulse was to go in and wait for her
and demand the explanation to all this; but without

even saying it to himself, he knew if he did this, if he pleaded ignorance, this girl would realize her mistake and keep silent. He was sure that it was his name that she feared, and the men associated with it.

And oddly, then, he thought of what a good name she had. Margot Curtin. He said it aloud, liking it.

CHAPTER FIVE

THE STABLEMAN had been right in his prediction, for Flood could see the Petrie men patrolling the streets in pairs with an open confidence that was an invitation to anything. The Palace was doing business again mainly with these Petrie men, since Hand's crew was not in evidence.

Flood's entry into the Palace was observed by every man in the room, and it was easy to see they were men alert for a quarrel. Petrie was forcing things, Flood guessed, and he admired him for it.

He singled out Petrie sitting at one of the poker tables talking to a swart, hard-bitten man whom Flood recognized as the one who, a half hour before, had warned him not to enter the saloon.

He angled over to Petrie's table, and immediately the men drinking at the bar ceased talking, turned and watched him. Petrie and his companion fell quiet, so that Flood's voice sounded rich and firm as he paused with a hand on the back of an empty chair at Petrie's table, and said, "I heard you might be looking for riders."

"Where'd you hear it?" the swart man asked, before Petrie could speak. There was the same truculence in his speech as in his manner, a sort of blunt invitation for men to dislike him. Hard of eye, squat, square of jaw, he stared at Flood from under the brim of a soiled Stetson that rode his squarish head at an arrogant angle. Flood accepted his stare with blank, careless good humor, and his answer was mild.

"Why, in plain fact, from Honeywell, the marshal."

Petrie chuckled at this, and his smile was pleasant, if slow and sparse. "I'm surprised he didn't deputize you. A man can't go in his office without being asked."

"He tried," Flood said.

"He'll pay you more than I will," Petrie said. "That is, if it's money you're after."

"It is. But not that kind."

"You'll get the same kind from me," Petrie replied. "Fighting wages. Or is it because you don't like to wear a badge while you earn it?"

"Maybe that's it," Flood said.

Petrie looked at his companion and laughed softly. "Sign him on, Breck."

Breck had not ceased staring at Flood, and now he made a quick gesture of interruption with his hand.

"I can't get it out of my mind I've seen you," he said. "You're new to this country?"

Flood nodded.

"That's funny," Breck continued, his tone tentative and calculating. "I've never been far from here either." His hard unblinking eyes were searching every line of Flood's face. "Your name," he said. "What is it?"

"Flood."

Breck leaned forward a little. "Flood, you say?" And when Flood nodded, he leaned back in his chair, and said, "Ah," softly.

Then he looked at Petrie and when Petrie gave no sign, he asked, "You couldn't have had a brother by the name of Gordon?"

Again Flood nodded.

"That was caught in a pretty nasty mess south of here some time ago?"

"Yes."

Breck was looking at Petrie now. Petrie picked up an empty glass sitting before him and laid it down again, his thin lips pursed, his head already moving in negation.

"I reckon our payroll is full," Breck said. "Maybe you better go back and see Honeywell."

"Maybe you better not," Petrie said quietly, looking up at Flood. "He'd ask you a lot of questions I'm not even going to." There was an amused smile on his long face, and behind the insolence in his eyes, Flood could see more amusement.

"Like what?" Flood asked curiously.

"They never did find that Munro herd Gordie was trying to steal," Petrie said gently. "They only got three men out of a dozen or so. Folks have got a long memory for things like that—a little too long for me to risk hiring you, Flood. I'm not loved around here. I have to be careful."

"Maybe that would be safer," Flood said, a trace of a smile on his face too.

He turned to go when Breck said, "Have you tried Hand yet?"

Flood paused in his stride. "Why would I?"

Breck laughed briefly. "The last Flood in these parts had a notion that Hand's Bar Stirrup brand looked better on our cattle than our own Wagon Hammer brand. His notion cost us a sizable bunch of calves. Hand liked him and his idea, though."

Flood walked back to the table and when he spoke his voice was gentle, his face still. "And you think he might like me for the same reason?"

"I never said so."

Flood leaned both hands on the table and looked at Breck. "If you think so, I would like to hear you say it."

Breck's face tautened a little so that it drew his eyes narrow, and he took his hands off the table. "I said, I never said so."

"Don't," Flood said. He stood erect, aware now of the silence in the room and of the men at the bar watching him. But he waited a moment for Breck to speak, and when he did not, Flood turned and walked slowly between the flanking rows of men to the door and went out. He had not noticed up till now that Honeywell had been standing just inside the door, listening. Honeywell fell in beside him.

"That's twice," the marshal said. "Breckenridge won't

forget, even if Petrie does, which isn't likely."

"Where will I find Hand?" Flood asked.

"Why do you want him?"

"I want to ride for him."

"Come along then," Honeywell said. "He's down at Sewell's place buying shells, if he has any sense."

Sewell's store lay down the street from the sheriff's office and they crossed the street together in silence, except for the heavy breathing of Honeywell.

When they were on the far sidewalk, Honeywell said pleasantly, "So you're Gordon Flood's brother. You make a mistake by admitting it."

Flood said, "I've never done a thing to make me change my name yet."

"That's not it. I'm kin to Jeff Davis, but I never said so outside of Texas."

Flood said, "A man is free to say he doesn't like it."

"That's the trouble. Some are apt to."

"Let them," Flood said.

The long, shelved room of Sewell's store was empty, except for Hand and two companions. Honeywell made the introductions, and Hand shook hands with Flood. There was a kind of stolid and deliberate unhaste in Hand's actions that was unlike Petrie. He introduced Flood to Wes Emory, the foreman of his Bar Stirrup, and Emory shook hands with a loose, casual diffidence. He was a slight man, yet tall, five years younger than Hand, and he had an amiable drawl that contrasted strangely with the gravity of his face and its look of sober responsibility. Morgan, the other hand, was a Bar Stirrup rider too, a pock-marked, silent man with evasive eyes and a loose, surly face.

Honeywell stated Flood's business. "He wants to ride for you, Ben."

Hand looked at the marshal, suspicion immediately in his face.

"Since when did you start sending riders to me, Sam? Or have you changed your mind about this quarrel?"

"No, I think you are fools, both of you. I came along with Flood to keep you from doing what Breckenridge did when Flood wanted to join up with the Wagon Hammer."

"And what was that?"

"He didn't like Flood's name, and told him so. He thought better of it when Flood asked for particulars. Do you like his name?"

Hand looked quietly at Flood. "I knew Gordie Flood. He was no good. Are you brothers?"

Flood nodded, reading only truth in Hand's speech.

"And you wanted to ride for the Wagon Hammer? Why?"

"Petrie was closest," Flood said indifferently.

"But he wouldn't take you. Is that it?" When Flood said it was, Hand continued, "And you want to ride for me, now, knowing what is coming on?"

"Yes."

"I'll pay you thirty a month and found," Hand said. "Will you work for that?"

"Yes."

Hand said to Honeywell, "If you say he's all right, Sam, I'll sign him on."

Honeywell's sad face broke into a sadder smile and he looked at Flood. "He had sense enough not to take a deputy's badge, Ben. I can't swear to anything but his good sense, and he'll be alone having that at the Bar Stirrup."

Hand smiled narrowly, both at the marshal and Flood. "All right, Flood. You'll do."

CHAPTER SIX

THEY RODE OUT OF TOWN to the west, Hand, Flood, Morgan and Emory. It was late afternoon now, and they traveled at a fast trot through a rolling country that was crossed by low timbered ridges and occasional shallow valleys. They rode abreast, Flood on the outside next to Hand, who pointed out an occasional landmark. Once he stopped at the corner of Bar Stirrup range

which was unmarked, and roughly outlined for Flood
the position and length of his range.

"And where is the Silver Creek range?" Flood asked,
when he had finished.

Hand's broad face became a little grimmer as he told
him. To the west a long valley knifed into the mountains at their lowest part. It was lush range, a good bit
of it salt grass that was a tonic to gaunt cattle after winter feeding. Year in, year out, the heavier snows of
winter missed it, so that it was good winter range too,
but by an unwritten agreement of the ranchers in the
country, it was grazed only in the summer.

"When I got to spreading out," Hand said slowly, "I
wanted that valley. We all grazed it because it was free
range and big enough for everyone. I was closest to it
and I needed it most, so I made a deal with the outfits
using it. I bought them out—with no title, of course,
since it's public domain. All but a few small outfits were
willing, and those I didn't bother with because they
didn't tally much. Then Petrie moved in on it. Not
only that, he organized a lot of the nester trash into
backing his play."

Here Hand's voice became dogged, and Flood noticed
his hands fisted as they rested on his saddle horn. "It
left me to remind Petrie of the bargain, but he claimed
it didn't touch him, since he had never agreed to my
having it. It was free range, and he would get his share
of it. I organized the men who were willing to stick to
their bargain, and who could see it was useless to make
any kind of contract if it could not be enforced. That's
the way it stands now, Petrie's cattle are on the range.
But I think we can take care of that. Maybe tonight."

Flood heard no more about the plans until they were
at the Bar Stirrup. The main building was a log affair
of one long room, a wing built on the south end which
was the bunkhouse. A cluster of sheds and corrals lay
off to the north at the edge of clearing. The timber cut
down close to the house in the rear. The whole faced a
saucerlike valley divided by a crudely bridged creek.

Seeing Flood look it over, Hand said, "It's not big."

"Then those weren't your men at the Palace," Flood said.

"A man has to depend on friends in a fix like this," Hand said. "They rode in with me today."

Unsaddling with Morgan and Emory in the dusk, Flood began to understand Hand's circumstances. Hand was a man in the process of spreading out his holdings, a man who lived like a hermit and expected his men to do the same. Every cent Hand made probably went back into more land and more cattle, so that he had neither the money nor the men to wage a range war of any magnitude. Rather, he depended on his neighbors and friends, those men who inevitably, as Honeywell had said, must take sides and abide by their leader.

Flood guessed he had been hired because he was a stranger, and because when a rancher hires a hand, he hires his unswerving loyalty and his life. Hand would need men like Flood, fighting men, men who would carry out his orders and not be hampered by considerations of family and money and personal gain, as these neighbors and friends would be. It was purely a business deal. Hand had hired a man with guns.

Flood was content with this, although he knew it would be long before he would be in Hand's confidence, or in the confidence of these Bar Stirrup men. His name was at once a sign and a warning, and he could see that Emory and Morgan, while they had said nothing, resented his being here. They would be wondering what had brought a brother of Gordon Flood to this country, and they would not trust him. But Flood kept telling himself that this was a toe hold, an introduction to this land where Shifflin's men and herds had disappeared, and that sooner or later he would turn up a clue to their vanishing.

Morgan and Emory finished unsaddling before he did, and went on to the house without a word. It was perhaps a natural act, but in it Flood read their indifference to him. He wondered if he would have to fight the indifference of all the men on this range before he got what he wanted, and thinking of this, he wondered idly if Hand might be the man he was looking for. But immediately he dismissed the thought. This was hardly the outfit of a man who made cattle stealing a business. He went on to the house alone.

Hand had a desk in a corner of the big main room, which contained a long table near a door letting out on to the cook shed. The floor was covered with gear— saddles, bridles, blankets, ropes, slickers, boxes and papers. Two rawhide easy chairs made up the rest of the furniture.

Hand was already at his desk, writing by candlelight. The lone lamp was on the long table, which was set for supper. Flood caught a glimpse of an old man in shirt sleeves out in the kitchen. Occasionally, this man would enter the room in his business, and look at Flood curiously.

Morgan, sorting over and putting away on a wall shelf the boxes of shells he had brought out from town in a gunny-sack, looked up from his work once and said to the cook, "Nosey, this here is Flood, a new hand."

Morgan watched Flood, who nodded and was nodded at in return by the cook, and over his small, pock-marked face there was a look of amusement his bending over did not hide. Emory was collecting guns from benches and corners and putting them in the wall gun rack at the rear of the room.

A few minutes later, at the cook's surly invitation to eat, Hand said, without looking up, "Go ahead."

Only when they were well into the meal did Hand leave his desk and sit down with them. He laid three notes by Morgan's plate, saying, "When you've eaten, take those to Golding, Sisson and Braid. After this, they'll either be with us or against us."

Emory looked up from his plate, his lined, somber face curious. "Does it say for them to meet us tonight?"

"Yes," Hand said.

Emory shook his head. "Then one of them will ride to Petrie with it sure."

"It will be too late for him to do anything, even if

they do," Hand said. He began eating with a keen hunger, and did not even look up as the cook slid into the seat at the end of the table.

A strange crew, Flood thought, regarding them covertly. Emory was probably a good head, loyal, but somehow lacking in the qualities that command men. The soiled, rumpled Nosey was probably the oldest hand here, and had been pensioned off to the kitchen. Morgan was anybody's guess, a petty little man who had an almost physical need for somebody to bully him around. Hardly the material with which to fight a range war, and apparently, Hand was preparing to begin hostilities this night.

Flood wasn't surprised then when Hand said to him toward the end of the meal, "Flood, you come along with Emory and me tonight."

But as Hand continued to eat, he kept staring absently at a point a little ahead of his plate, and Flood had the impression that he was still uncertain of the night's plans. When he began to quiz Emory, Flood was sure of it.

"Find out about the location of that Wagon Hammer stuff on the Silver Creek?"

"A couple of the boys in town said they'd seen the herd at the north end, like we wanted."

Hand nodded. "I heard that too. It must be so." He frowned, then asked, "How many Petrie men did you hear were riding herd?"

"Four."

Hand acted as if he did not hear this, but presently he said, "That's mighty few men for a herd that size if a man is expecting trouble. Surely Petrie is."

Emory ceased eating and put down his fork. "I wouldn't do it, Ben. It's got a queer look."

Hand only looked up at him, but did not stop eating.

Emory went on. "Petrie has run enough cattle on that Silver Creek range to know the bad spots. He knows that bog is there. I've seen Wagon Hammer riders pulling stuff out of it. If Petrie expects trouble, then he's not going to leave a herd close to that bog to be stampeded into it—not unless he wants to, that is. He's not the man to stick his neck out."

"That's bait, Ben," Nosey said, not even looking up from his plate.

"Maybe," Hand conceded. "It won't hurt to find out."

Nosey said flatly, "For a man that aims to keep a bunch of these small outfits on his side, you ain't talking sense, Ben."

"Why not?"

"Because tonight you'll take two of your own riders and three from your neighbors. If you walk into trouble, somebody will get hurt, maybe bad. If you get your neighbors shot up, you'll find they've cooled off considerable the next time you want them to ride with you."

Flood had finished eating now, and he was filling his pipe, observing the slow course of the argument. He could see this doubt take hold in Hand's mind, and it occurred to him that this was the way the Bar Stirrup was used to running its affairs—by argument. But he was fairly certain that Hand would override the others in the end.

Nosey rose with his plate and went into the kitchen, pausing at the door long enough to say to Hand, "All things even, Ben, the man that wins this fight will be the man that loses his own paid riders and makes the other man lose his friends. I've seen enough of these to know."

Hand paused a moment to consider this and then resumed eating. He said to Emory, "You'll do what I say."

"Sure," Emory said. "I'll even steal the herd if you want me to."

Morgan was finished now, and he leaned back to pick his teeth. Seeing the notes before him, he pocketed them.

Suddenly Hand looked at Flood and said, "What do you think, Flood?"

"I'm not sure I understand it all," Flood said evasively.

"There's a bog over in the south corner of that Silver

Creek range," Hand began. "Petrie's got cattle close to it, four men riding herd. I plan to take my men and stampede the herd into that bog. With any luck, he'll lose half the herd. Tomorrow, when his whole crew is working trying to pull the stuff out, I'll run him clean off the Silver Creek range. What do you think of it?"

"I think that's just what he wants you to do," Flood said.

Hand laid his fork down. "Why would he want me to do it?"

Flood shrugged. "Maybe I'm not the one to say. I don't know the country."

"Go ahead," Hand said. "I'd like to hear why Petrie wants me to drive his stuff into that bog."

Flood said, "Because while you are doing that, he'll probably take the rest of his crew and steal every head of stuff you own." He paused, then said, "Is it true that one of these men who are getting your notes will go to Petrie with it?"

"I think so. Sisson probably," Hand said slowly.

"All right. There's the evidence Petrie wants. He'll have it in writing, this evidence that you were calling men together to make trouble for him. All he's got to do is make a lot worse trouble for you that same night, and when Mayhew hears about it, Petrie will have the proof that you started it. Nobody will blame him for revenging himself on you."

Nosey, who had been standing in the kitchen doorway, grunted approval. "There's a man that will outguess Petrie, Ben."

"How do you know this will happen?" Hand asked slowly, his tone puzzled.

Flood shrugged. "I don't. That's what I would do in Petrie's place. He puts this herd of his by the bog without enough riders. It's an easy bit of trouble for you to make him, so you ride out with your men to do it. Meanwhile, he takes his men, steals your herds, stampedes them or destroys them."

Hand leaned back in his chair now and rolled a smoke with deliberate studied reflection.

Emory, watching Hand hopefully, said, "There's only Coe up'at the Brush Creek line camp. He couldn't fight off all Petrie's crew."

Hand ignored this, and said to Flood, "What would you do, then?"

"Send those notes like you planned, and let one of them reach Petrie. Then don't show up at the Silver Creek range. Ride over to your own herds and wait. When Petrie shows up there, you can give him all the trouble he wants. It's his own medicine."

Hand smashed his cigarette on the table top and stood up. "You're right. That's what he'll do, and that's what I'll do." He looked at Flood now, with a new respect in his eyes. "I've got one thing to thank Petrie for," he said grimly, a trace of a smile on his face. "He didn't hire you."

Morgan was instructed to deliver the first note to Sisson immediately. Emory was to ride over and pick up the three neighboring cattlemen Hand had chosen to ride with him that night. Hand and Flood would ride immediately to the Brush Creek line camp to join Coe, the fourth and remaining Bar Stirrup hand. Nosey was to remain here and guard the place.

At the corral, Hand was first saddled, and he rode up beside Morgan, who was near the lantern. "When you've got those notes delivered, come back here to pick up Nosey. Then both of you ride up to the line camp. Bring plenty of shells."

CHAPTER SEVEN

HAND AND FLOOD CUT INTO THE TIMBER behind the house. If Hand was a man slow to act, he was thorough and quick in action. They crossed a dozen open parks and timbered ridges before they stopped to blow their horses, and then Hand seemed reluctant to take the time. They were climbing steadily, moving into more broken country under the peaks where Hand picked up a creek whose course they followed, making their climb easier.

Once, where the creek widened on a flat, Hand stopped. He raised a hand that halted Flood and they both listened. Flood picked out the sound of horses, and Hand pulled his horse into the brush along the creek while Flood moved into the fringing timber.

A long moment later, three riders forded the creek. The last horse wanted to drink and stopped, but was cursed and pulled up and was soon gone into the timber with the others.

Hand only grunted. They held to the creek until the banks were steepened by the crowding hills. Hand then angled up on a long climb through thick timber that brought them out at the edge of level open country. He hugged the edge of this until they saw a light, when he cut straight across to it. A few scattered head of cattle moved away from them in the night.

Coe evidently heard their horses, for the light went out before they reached the shack. Hand called to him and he came out.

"Anything wrong, Ben?" he greeted Hand.

"Plenty. This is Flood, a new hand." When they had shaken hands, Hand said, "Saddle up."

Hand evidently seemed certain of his objective. He asked Coe a few questions as to where the cattle would be bunched, and was told that since being pushed to higher range the week before, they were working steadily down to the Salt Lick, from where Coe intended to move them soon.

"Seen any strange horse tracks around the Lick?" Hand asked.

"Yes. Yesterday. Fresh ones." Coe had a deliberate, warm voice that made Flood wish the night was not so thick, and that he could see something besides a rather burly, squat man on a big horse who understood things without being told.

Hand either thought the time was too short to wait for reinforcements, or he had forgotten them. They sloped down to the north and east at a gallop now. Beside a small stream that dropped over the lip of a ridge, Hand pulled up.

"What will they do, Coe?"

"I know what I'd do in his place," Coe said slowly. "The cattle are at the lick at the upper end of Salt Basin. If I once got the cattle on the move and in order, I'd push them straight east the three miles to the Copper Canyon breaks. I don't think it can be done, though, because the cattle will likely mill and stampede. So he'll likely string his men out to push them over the low ridge on the north side of the basin. Once over that, they've got a downhill drag to the Brush Creek gully. It's not much of a gully, but a big bunch of cattle could pile up in it pretty high. They'd break legs, and a steer with a broken leg is as good as a dead steer."

"Go ahead, then," Hand said.

Coe moved on through a scattering of sparse timber until they were at the base of a low hogback, then he angled and hugged the slope for perhaps a quarter of a mile. Here he turned his horse and climbed the ridge. Once atop it, where it looked over the broad tilting expanse of Salt Basin, they did not have time to blow their horses before a stutter of shots racketed down from far up the slope.

Almost immediately from the base of the hogback below them, several riders pulled out of the shadow and started north at a brisk trot, already in single file. Darkness made the open stretch before them blurred and smooth, a great grassy tableland that tilted west and north to the black horizon.

Then they heard the first warning rumble of the herd in motion.

"This will be heard," Coe said, more to Flood than to Hand. "Those cattle are coming our way downhill. Petrie's riders will fan and try to throw them north. All we can do is keep riders off the lead steers, so this stampede will keep its course past them. Once free, they'll run themselves out down the basin."

"Take out where you like, Flood," Hand said, and turned his horse down the slope.

Flood followed them until they were on the level, then he angled sharply to the north at right angles to the sound, and spurred his gray. If he could get on the other side of this oncoming wedge of cattle, he could make it twice as difficult for Petrie to turn the herd.

He picked out the first rifle shot, which ripped over the rumble of the stampede in vicious peroration. He guessed that might be Hand, and he remembered oddly that courage always seemed a part of simple men like Hand who loved a fight more than guile.

Then he saw a tangle of gunfire ahead, and wheeled his horse. The first dark blot of lead cattle surged out of the night and he swung toward it, relieved that he had judged the course fairly well by its sound.

It took a moment for his horse to reach the traveling speed of the herd, and then he edged him closer in and spurred him. In the lead a dozen burly steers were in single file. Flood worked toward the leader, swinging up his six-gun in his right hand.

Then, from over the backs of these steers on their far side, a rider opened fire and the cattle swerved toward Flood. His first three shots were in the faces of the lead steers, who, obedient to their unleashed fear, swerved back into their course. And then Flood lifted his gun and shot twice at the dark, racing figure beyond the cattle. He heard a man curse wildly and then scream and then there was a milling and grunting and bawling as cattle piled up, wave after wave, on the downed rider's horse and then rushed on.

Flood loaded his gun again and shot at the ground in front and to one side of the lead steers and again they swung away from him. He looked up and saw the dark peninsula of the hogback close now on the other side of the cattle. Checking his horse a little, he swung out and the cattle flowed past him, free now to run themselves out.

A rider loomed out of the night behind him and jogged toward him.

"You've done that before."

It was Coe, and before Flood could answer, he said,

"Ben is back there."

Riding free against the tide of the herd, it did not take long for the cattle to pass them. And on the dying sound of their running came the snarl of gunfire far ahead.

Flood made out an island of trees and brush in the sea of grass. Along its length, men were shooting at spaced intervals. And far out on the level, there was a dark smudge from which gunfire was issuing too, but this was from a single man—Hand probably.

Coe pulled up, and Flood said, "I'd like to see if they wouldn't flush out in the open."

Coe chuckled. "I think they will. Let's try it."

They swung in a wide circle and came up behind the brushy island, their approach deadened by the grass and the clatter of gunfire. Coe took the far end and crashed into the brush, his gun blasting.

Flood took the near end, hardly as cautious.

His gray's first lunge put them deep in the thicket, and Flood heard the gun closest him cease firing and some muted bitter words, then more bitter words as a man fought a horse and they both crashed clear. He turned his horse at right angles down the middle, shooting occasionally. When his gun was empty, he pulled his carbine from the boot and rested it across his saddle, but the brush was so thick he holstered it again and was content with the noise he made.

Then from his right he heard someone speak and he pulled up short.

"Oh, damn, damn!" a voice said, and a horse snorted. Flood sat rigid in his saddle. He knew that voice, and would always know it. It was Margot Curtin's! When it said frantically to the night, "Won't somebody help me with him quick?" He dismounted and fought the brush until he heard the horse snort and tramp again, close to him now.

He shouldered through a few yards farther and saw the horse. He seized its bridle and the girl's voice, almost beside him, said, "Who is it?"

"You fool," Flood said thickly. "Get out of here!"

There was a pause and then the girl said faintly, "Oh!"

The tempo of Hand's firing had increased now as he was taking the last wild shots at the riders fleeing the brush.

"But you must help me!" the girl pleaded. "He is shot."

Flood heard a rustle in the brush at his feet and instinctively he dodged just as a gun crashed a yard from him on the floor of the thicket.

He dived for it, almost under the horse's feet and feeling a gun which he seized and then the arm and then the body, he slugged short and hard where the face was. He hit it. Standing up, breathing hard, he reached out to quiet the horse, saying, "Is that why you wouldn't leave?"

"Yes," the girl said humbly. "Are you hit?"

Flood only said, "Take a short grip on that bridle and hold it."

He reached down and picked up the limp body at his feet and, although it was heavy and solid, he slung it over the saddle, making adjustments so it would stay. Then he brushed the girl out of the way and pulled the horse around and lead it beyond the brush.

"Flood!" Coe's voice called from the other side of the thicket.

The girl was by him now. Flood said, "If he's hurt bad, hole up in the timber till daylight."

"Yes," she said softly. "I—I'm sorry Loosh shot at you. He didn't know, I swear he didn't."

"Yes," Flood said coldly, knowing for sure now what he had guessed at when he threw the body across the saddle. This man was Petrie. Flood left her and walked into the thicket, calling, "Coe."

Coe answered and Flood found his horse and rode out. He discovered that he was furiously angry and he fought it down, so that when he joined Coe and they trotted over to Hand, he seemed calm as usual.

"That was a beautiful thing to see," Hand said with deliberate praise. "All of it."

Coe chuckled. "How many were there?"

"Five in the thicket. Eight altogether. Petrie was with them, too. I heard his voice."

Flood's thought shuttled to the girl. She was Petrie's woman, loyal enough to stick by him when he needed her. And for some reason, Flood knew Hand could never be told this, and that it must be his secret.

He recalled the meeting with her that afternoon, remembered that this Margot Curtin had thought him a killer gunman and pleaded for mercy from him and his men. And, his memory noted swiftly, she was Petrie's woman. Petrie hated Hand, too, and she would hate him, Flood, now, because he was a Bar Stirrup rider—hate him more for what he had just now done. He silently cursed all the twisted circumstances that seemed to make this girl his enemy, and after he had done it, he wondered why he should care at all.

He was aware now that Hand was asking him a question, so he said, "What?"

"I say, did they get any cattle over to the gully? Listen to that bawling."

Flood listened and he could hear a muted, measured bawling down the slope. Then he recalled.

"A rider went down in the stampede," Flood said. "They piled up on him."

"Then he's dead and they'll get him," Hand said. "We better clear out before they discover how many we are." Then he said casually, "I'm hit. I haven't got a horse either."

Not daring to light a match, Coe examined his wound. A slug had cut the flesh at the base of Hand's neck where it joined the shoulder. It was bloody, but not dangerous, and Coe bandaged it as best he could with his handkerchief, then gave Hand his horse and mounted behind him.

Flood said, "I hate to leave those cattle hurt and piled up there."

"Let them go," Hand said. "As soon as they miss their man, they'll be back. They'll kill the cattle. I don't want you going back, Flood. It's too dangerous."

They set out for the shack, silent now.

CHAPTER EIGHT

WHEN THERE WAS ENOUGH LIGHT TO SEE, Margot left Petrie and went down to the edge of the timber. Her examination of the shallow stretch of basin where the stampede had run its course during the night was brief. It served to erase some of the hysteria in her face, however, and crowd into the back of her mind the long nightmare she had gone through in bringing Petrie back to consciousness.

When she returned, Petrie asked, "What did you see?"

He was propped against a rock on a slicker near the trickle of stream in the thick timber. There was a damp rag on the side of his face and over his ear, and he was holding it there with smoldering impatience. His worn denim trousers were spotted with blood, as was his flannel shirt, and he was shivering regularly and could not stop it.

"There are some cattle piled up far down near that jut of rock," she said, watching him with grave eyes.

"A horse with them?"

"I couldn't see." She came to his side and knelt. "Loosh, can't I build a fire? You are so cold you're blue. Do you know how long you lay on the ground here completely unconscious? Can't I build one?"

"No. We can't take the chance." He laid a big hand over hers and smiled briefly, wanly. "I was a fool to let you come with me last night, but I'll not be fool enough to let you watch them kill me." When she did not answer, he said, "I'm sorry, darling."

She watched him look away through the trees, and she studied his face in taut repose. It was a good face, she thought, but how little she could read it, and how stupid it was to think of it as a badge where a man

showed all his character for the world to judge. It would
have a scar now, a deep furrow running from cheekbone
to ear. Yet in a way, it was a face she understood: narrow, with the flesh leaned off the muscle lines, burned
to a permanent gold color, shades darker than the fine
flaxen hair. The mouth was thin-lipped and wide, best
when it suddenly smiled. The eyes were dark and
febrile, quick as the intelligence behind them, which
often astonished and always pleased her. But these eyes
needed a deeper setting in his skull, and they should
have been blue, she thought. And this reminded her of
her own eyes, and then of Flood's, which she had noticed were so like hers.

She flushed then, thinking of Flood's hot and violent
anger of last night, when he found her there in the
brush. Had he known it was Loosh that he slung over
the saddle and ordered her to take off? She doubted it,
but she believed he would have acted the same even if
he had known.

Unconsciously now, she contrasted Flood with Loosh.
They were about the same height, but Flood moved
with an indolent, contained grace that Loosh did not
have. Perhaps that was because Flood was a gunman,
a man used to being only a quick movement from death,
she thought. Flood's face had a carved, squarish cast,
and he seemed to speak and retire and understand with
those eyes while his face remained unchanged and somber. Maybe its soberness was because of the deep weathered brown of his skin, or of the wide and unsmiling
mouth.

She thought of his body too, not as big as Petrie's,
but tighter knit, straight, flat, covered with worn and
common clothes that could not hide the elegance of
movement. His shoulders were neither hulking nor mas-
sive, like Loosh's. But he was a gunman, she told herself,
a hired killer, in spite of his kindness to her last night.
Yet hadn't Loosh only a moment ago sworn to kill
Flood? What was the difference between the two, except
that Flood was franker? And thinking this, seeing herself take Flood's part, she flushed again with a secret

shame. She brushed a strand of hair from her forehead.

"Loosh," she said. He looked at her. "Is it your pride that won't let us ride out of here? Are you afraid you are so weak you will faint?"

"No," Petrie answered, smiling. "It's not that. Hand will have men out this morning, pushing his cattle up where he thinks they'll be safer. I have six shells left, and my head feels split wide open. It's risky. If we wanted to go, we should have done it right after the fight. But then we couldn't."

"Would you go now if you were alone?"

"Yes."

"But if I came with you last night, I should take all the chances with you, too."

"No. Breck will be here soon. He's in these hills now hunting them for me."

"But you are lying here blue with cold," Margot said, trying to ease her conscience. "You are fretting about everything, too—wondering if you've lost any men and who they were."

"Not that," Petrie said, looking away. "I'm blaming myself for misjudging Hand." Then he corrected himself. "No, not Hand either. It was Flood that did that. I wish I had killed him."

Margot sat utterly still on the boulder behind Petrie. Then she said quietly, "He saved your life."

"Yes. Still, I wish I had killed him."

She watched his head, and her hands were nervously pleating and unpleating the heavy gabardine skirt she wore. Suddenly, they stilled.

"That's rotten, Loosh," she said, almost vehemently. "It's not like you."

He twisted his head up to look at her. "I've got a cheekbone nicked, half an ear shot away, and for good measure I was slugged in the face. I've had my men hurt and my plans trampled. If that man Flood had not joined up with the Bar Stirrup I wouldn't have any of this. I'm a simple man, Margot. Because Flood was weak enough to hit me instead of shoot me, it doesn't change things. I don't want it to. I say I wish I had killed him. I will."

"Why is he here?" she asked.

Petrie looked away from her. "That's not important."

"But why is he?"

"I can't imagine, unless Hand sent for him."

"But you say he asked you to take him on."

"He knew I wouldn't. That was a bluff, so he could go to Hand innocently. I can use riffraff at a time like this, but not a man with his name."

"Tell me again about his brother," Margot asked softly.

"I never saw him, but I know his name stinks. He and a gang of men stole a S. S. Munro trail herd of three thousand cattle a year or so ago, down near the Point Loma badlands. Flood was caught and killed, and a good job, too."

"Three thousand cattle," Margot said softly. "And they never found them?"

"No."

"Where could they have gone?"

"A thousand places." He looked up at her. "Why are you so interested?"

"I don't know," she said gravely. "I've ridden with you through those badlands. That's where you told me the story. They flank the high mountains, where cattle couldn't be crossed. I've been in the country on both sides of the badlands. I don't understand where they could have gone."

"Maybe Hand could tell."

"Why do you say that, Loosh?" Margot asked swiftly.

"Prejudice," Petrie answered frankly. "He knew Gordon Flood. He's hired Mark Flood. He's a range hog and money mad, and crooked in the bargain. Why couldn't he?"

Margot rose and took the cloth from Petrie's face, wet it in the stream, then placed it on his face again. He smiled his thanks, but she knew he was thinking of other things and that suddenly he had lost his need of her, as all men do of women when they are off to the wars. Its unreasonableness angered her.

"You look hideous," she said.

Petrie understood a little of this, and he smiled. "I know. I thought to protect you, and here it has ended by my being saved by you."

"Not by me. By the man you want to kill."

"Damn that man," Petrie said calmly. "He wouldn't shoot a down man. But once I'm on horseback again, he'll try to gun me like the killer he is. Why shouldn't I do the same?"

"You shot at him last night, when he couldn't see you."

Petrie laughed. "Margot, this is going around in a circle. Flood is a killer, a saddle-tramp, who offered to take killer's wages from me or anybody that would hire him. I'm at war with Hand, and Flood is Hand's brains. He's got to go if I'm to survive, the same as Hand must go. That's unpleasant and elemental, but it's so."

Margot rose, and said, "I'll look again."

This time, when she reached the edge of the timber, she saw two men working at the carcasses of the cattle, their horses ground-haltered at a distance. Two riders were headed for the timber, where one more was already slowly riding the edge. They were Wagon Hammer men, and she whistled, and when they heard her and waved, she turned back to Petrie.

"Breck is coming."

Petrie sat up, pain draining the color from his face. "Can you get this bandaged?"

Breckenridge rode up just as she was finishing, and Petrie did not even greet him, nor the two men who came with him.

"They got Kenney," Breck said, then, "What happened to you?"

"They got me too," Petrie said calmly. "Not bad, though. What happened to Kenney?"

"His horse was shot from under him and he was tramped to—he fell in front of the cattle."

Margot stood up. "Can you get him home, Breck? And in heaven's name, give him your jacket."

Breck peeled a windbreaker from his shoulders and

gave it to Petrie, and helped him to stand up and put it on.

"Shall I send Doc Carew out to your place?" Margot asked him.

"No. They'll think I'm hurt. Where are you going?"

"Home."

"Cliff, ride with her," Petrie said to one of the men.

"No. I'm going alone." She turned and walked over to where her horse was tied down creek, and mounted and rode off. Petrie watched her go, and he seemed unworried.

After a pause, Breck said, "We hunted half the night for you, Loosh. God, I—"

"I know," Petrie said impatiently. "What else happened?"

Breck swore bitterly. "Nothing. We'd of got Hand if they hadn't smoked us out from behind."

"That was Flood," Petrie said. "No Bar Stirrup riders were killed?"

"Not that I know of."

"Good," Petrie said gently. "How bad a shape—no. Is it possible to move Kenney?"

"I'd shove dirt over what's left of him," Breck said, his distaste evident.

"I don't mean that. Is it possible to move his body?"

"Yes. In a slicker," Breck said slowly, searching Petrie's face.

"Help me up."

Breck gave him an arm and then assisted him to his horse and watched him mount.

"Do you think you could get Kenney over by that Silver Creek bog?" Petrie asked.

Breck looked down at the ground, and Petrie said sharply, "Answer, man. Can you?"

"I reckon."

"Then you do it. Shove about fifty head of our stuff in the bog and lay—lay Kenney on the ground close." He paused. "If you can, drive them—no, don't do that. Lay him on the ground. I'll do the rest."

"Bury him, you mean?"

"No. I'm riding into town now. I'll see if Mayhew will serve the warrant I am going to swear out against Hand."

"What for?"

"Kenney's murder."

Breck scowled. "That's all right, only we was on Bar Stirrup land stampeding Bar Stirrup cattle. What about that?"

Petrie smiled sardonically. "Were we? Perhaps we were. Kenney, though, was riding night herd on our stuff near the bog when he was shot and his body tromped by stampeding cattle that somebody was trying to bog."

Breck's smile was slow and understanding. "And who done this stampeding?" he asked, in the mock spirit of catechizing.

"We identified Hand's horse. The four night herders will swear to that, besides the six men we had in the hills that drove the Bar Stirrup riders off. Maybe you better send four new men out there and have those witnesses in to talk to me when I get back from telling this to Mayhew."

"That's risky, Loosh," Breck said, suddenly grave. "Flood will blow the lid off this fight faster than we can catch it if we do this."

"No. If I know Flood, he might do that, but I think he'll do this. If Hand goes to jail, Flood will steal him blind and jump the country. If he doesn't, we can take care of that too."

"Yes," Breck said, looking Petrie squarely in the eye, his word a question.

"Not yet," Petrie said, and rode off.

CHAPTER NINE

EMORY, his two companions, Morgan and Nosey, were all after the stampeded cattle by sunup, leaving the others to sleep. They had left shortly after Coe, Hand

and Flood got there.

But Flood was awake at daylight, and he got up. He walked over to Hand's bunk and looked down at him in the feeble light of dawn. There was a kind of unconquerable dignity in Hand even in sleep, and Flood studied his face. It seemed no different, no more relaxed than when he was awake. He moved a little in his sleep and his breathing was irregular, and Flood guessed it was the dull pain of his wound.

Flood turned away from him with a sudden feeling of impotence. Hand was a thick man and a dull one, but there was a solidity, an unassuming plainness coupled with a tenacity of purpose in him that Flood could not help but like. He could see how a nimble-witted person would despise Hand, but a wise one would never underestimate him.

He looked over at Coe sleeping on the dirt floor, and he found Coe watching him. There was no expression on Coe's honest, rough face; Flood got only the impression of watchful reserve.

Flood looked again at Hand.

"Queer," he said reflectively. "Most men look weak and defenseless in sleep. He doesn't."

Coe smiled a little. "Some day, I think he hopes he can do without it." He sat up now and reached for his boots and paused when he had them on. "But make no mistake, Flood. His stubborn way will get him what he wants. It always has. In the end, Petrie will find that out."

"Yes," Flood said, putting on his boots. He was thinking of the loyalty Coe had given Hand, a man ten years younger. When, a few hours ago, Flood had stepped into the lighted cabin and he and Coe looked at each other, they had become instant friends. There was that patience and reserve in Coe's face that Flood had seen in men who work best with animals and yet do not consider them better than humans. Short, barrel-big, with not an ounce of fat on him, there was a tranquillity, a look of utter peace in Coe's plain face that Flood placed immediately. He was a man truly born to serve, to be loyal and steady and honest and content with little; a man who is lost without a master. He had found one in Hand, and Flood thought more of Hand after seeing Coe.

Flood went out. There was cool, clean light outside and his gaze lifted to the peaks whose highest juts had already caught the bright wash of the sun.

"I think I'll ride," Flood said.

"Why not?" Coe said. "Emory will be back before Ben is awake."

"Like to come?" Flood asked. He smiled a little, but did not look at Coe. "As long as I'm fighting for a range, I'd like to see it."

Coe said he did. Without breakfast, they saddled up and took to the timber south. Their conversation bridged long silences, and yet Flood was finding out what he wanted. Coe told him a little of Petrie, and of his start. Petrie was the son of a prospector who died when Petrie was no more than a boy. The old man left him a little money, far too little to start him in ranching. But Petrie had taken the money and ridden south. That was in late winter. By the end of the next summer, he returned, driving a small trail herd of scrubby, scabby cows that he had culled from the Texas herds. It was a start, for land here was open and there was good range to spare.

It was the story of a provident man. In ten years, he had built his brand into one of the biggest in the country.

"And that's the trouble," Coe said. "If he was content to make it one of the biggest, men could live with him. But he wants it to be *the* biggest. He's got everything now that any man wants, but that's his blind spot."

"Does he want a wife?" Flood asked presently.

"He'll get one," Coe said. "That is, if he lives long enough." He rode a while without talking, then said, "And that will be the biggest injury he has done anybody yet."

"To the girl, you mean?"

"Yes."

"The Curtin girl, isn't it?"

Coe nodded and looked at him. "You've found out a lot of things about us, Flood, all mighty quick."

"I couldn't help that," Flood said. "It was—well, forced on me last night."

"I wondered if you'd tell that," Coe said calmly.

"You know?"

"Yes. When you stopped shooting, I rode through the brush and back along the other side. I heard the shot. I heard you tell her to get him out." He looked at Flood now. "You spared his life, Flood, when most men would have taken it. He'll never forgive you for that."

"I know," Flood said thoughtfully. "When he shot, I should have run."

The sun was well up when they crossed the long mesa that put them on the edge of the Silver Creek range. At the lip of the mesa they dismounted. The whole sweep of the Silver Creek range lay before them. Broad, hardly broken except by an alder-flanked creek, it sloped deep and wide up into the mountains. At its far end, it tilted up to a deep notch between high peaks. At its open end, the land dropped away into breaks that opened out eventually into the rolling grasslands of the range below.

"It's worth fighting for," Coe said.

And it was. The dark pine-clad mountains shouldered up all around it, their deep green giving its grass a pale sheen as of frost on a vast meadow. Flood looked again at the deep notch, and said, "What's on the other side of those peaks?"

"A town, they say. And mining camps."

"Is that a pass through the peaks to the town?" Flood asked, indicating the notch.

Coe considered a minute, then said, "It might be. I've never heard of it being used."

Flood looked at him sharply, but Coe was still considering the peaks. Here was the first tangible evidence of where Shifflin's herd might have gone. If this was a pass, then an army of cattle could be filtered through it to vanish from these men's sight. Flood thought back to something Hand had said, and he wondered if he should ask the question he wanted to. He decided he would.

"Didn't Hand say that Petrie's stuff is on this range now?"

Coe said yes.

"But if Hand claims it, why aren't his cattle here?"

"If a man is fighting for a garden, he doesn't have to fight in it, does he?"

"No, I see that," Flood said. "Yet, having it would strengthen Hand."

"I doubt it. When this fight blows up, the man who has his cattle out of the way and spread out will be less hampered by having to watch them. Because revenge is easiest when there are herds to destroy. When there aren't, then the quarrel centers between men." He gestured out toward Silver Creek. "Petrie's herd out there is small, just enough to assert his ownership. Most of his cattle are back deep in his range."

Flood weighed this and saw the truth in it. Still, he wondered. This Silver Creek range took on a new significance to him when he thought of that notch, and what it would mean to the man who owned it. And somehow, without putting it into words, he felt that this pass, not the miles of salt grass, was what lay behind the quarrel. Before, he had believed the thief could be any man who could command men to help him plunder the herd. Now, he believed Shifflin's killer was either Petrie or Hand, and that one of them was fighting for this pass and cloaking his end by naming it a fight for grass. He wondered which man it was, and he confessed to himself he did not know.

"I'd like to see it closer," Flood said.

"We can go down then."

Once in the high grass of the valley, they headed toward the creek and mountains. Beyond the creek, they entered some rolling country, and Coe said, "I'd go careful, here. Emory said Petrie had a herd somewhere close here."

Flood wanted only to look at the country, and he

offered to turn back, but Coe said with grim humor, "Be damned to that. We'll ride where we please."

They encountered occasional cattle now, but Coe ignored them, saying they were Petrie's and what of it. Topping a sharp rise, they pulled up to look at the country, but the first thing they saw were three men riding abreast at an angle to them a quarter mile off.

They were seen immediately, and there was a brief conference among the three below. Then they turned and started for Flood and Coe.

"That's Mayhew," Coe said, and in a second he added, "Mayhew, Honeywell and Petrie."

Flood said nothing, but looked at Coe questioningly.

"Stand your ground," Coe said. He reached down and loosened the Colt in his holster, and then slid it back and sat there waiting.

Mayhew was on a big bay that took the lead up the gentle slope. The sheriff greeted Coe with careless familiarity and nodded agreeably to Flood. Honeywell nodded to include both, as did Petrie, who had a neat bandage over part of his face and the side of his head. He observed Flood quietly, then looked away.

Coe looked them over and smiled a little when he saw the horse Honeywell was riding. It was a small Roman nosed sorrel, impatient at the weight imposed on it.

Coe said, "Sam, I'm willing to bet you trade ponies with Mayhew or carry that thing home on your back."

"I won't do either if he finds a low tree," the marshal said gravely, and without humor.

Coe looked at Mayhew. "What is it, Max?"

"We're taking a ride up yonder a ways. I thought maybe you'd like to go with us."

"Should I?" Coe said mildly.

"I reckon."

Coe looked at Petrie and smiled slightly. "All right."

They rode abreast, Coe and Flood next each other. There was an elaborate casualness about the two law men that neither Coe nor Flood missed. When they had ridden on a mile, they came upon a scattered herd of

Wagon Hammer cattle feeding. Two riders on the other side of the herd came toward them, and Flood saw one was Breckenridge. Coe said evenly to the sheriff, "I hope you know what you're doing, Max."

The sheriff only grunted. When Breckenridge approached, he looked first at Coe and Flood and then at Petrie, who asked, "Where is he, Breck?"

"Over by the creek."

"Where are the men?"

Breckenridge looked again at Coe and Flood. "Pulling bog."

Flood had an instinctive feeling that this was a piece of quiet theatrics, but he could not understand it yet. Petrie turned toward the creek, which made a sharp bend toward them here. Breckenridge pulled up short of the low alders lining the creek bank and dismounted. Mayhew, Honeywell, Petrie and the Wagon Hammer rider followed him.

"You better come along," Mayhew said to Coe. Flood and he dismounted and only then did Breckenridge kneel and pull something from under the alders—something that was wrapped in two soggy slickers.

"You won't want to look at this," Breck said.

He flipped the slicker back long enough for them to see and then covered it again. Honeywell turned around and spat.

Mayhew said, "Uh-huh."

Coe looked fleetingly at Flood and then he said to Petrie, "That must have been a nasty bundle to pack all that way."

"It wasn't far," Petrie said evenly. "Just up around the bend where the bog starts. Pulling him out of the ground was the hardest."

Coe said sharply, "You lie."

Mayhew whirled, so that he was facing Flood and Coe, and in between Petrie and Coe.

"Maybe you two better put your guns on the ground, Coe," he said mildly.

Coe said, "Let's all do it."

Petrie unbuckled his belt and let it fall to the ground,

then instructed Breck and the other Wagon Hammer rider to do the same. They stepped away from them, and Petrie said, "Remember, Mayhew, I didn't ask these men. You wanted the proof."

"I still do," Mayhew said. Flood and Coe took off their belts and Mayhew turned to his horse.

"Let's ride up and look."

Only as they were mounting did Flood hear for the first time the measured bawling of cattle. Petrie struck back from the creek toward a slight rise, which he followed, once on top.

A few hundred yards more and Flood could see that the ground just below the rise was bog. It fell away from the creek in level grass, but occasionally he caught the flash of sun on water in the midst of the grass there. As they rode farther, he could see where the bog held great black scars of mud. From these scars to the rise, the grass was pressed flat, where riders had dragged the cattle from the mire.

Then ahead, he saw two punchers at work. One was down in the mire, freeing and tying up the legs of a steer, while the other mounted puncher was waiting with a slack rope to drag the steer, once free, from the bog. They stopped work when they saw the others. Flood guessed there were fifty head bogged down in this area, and a few of them were bawling in blasts as measured as the ticking of a clock.

Petrie pulled up. "Here is the place. Maybe Tim better tell it. He was here."

The Wagon Hammer rider was young, taciturn and perfectly calm. He pointed to a spot down the bank and into the bog that was tromped into a snarl of watery mud and grass.

"Kenney was on this side when we heard the first shots. He tried to clear out and didn't make it. They caught him almost free and took him with them." He looked at Mayhew. "That's how we figured it, because we didn't miss him right then. When Hand rode off—"

"When who rode off?" Coe interrupted.

The rider looked at him. "It was Hand's voice and

Hand's horse. Figure it out any way you like."

"Go on," Mayhew said.

"Let's don't," Coe cut in. "I was with Hand all night. We weren't three miles from our Brush Creek line camp."

"You weren't either, I suppose," Mayhew said to Flood.

"Maybe Petrie could verify that," Flood said, with a nod.

"Yes. I was there," Petrie said. "I didn't see or hear Hand, though."

"What were you doing there, Loosh?" Honeywell asked gently.

"I was driving Hand's stuff clear out of the country," Petrie said flatly. "I told him I would. I told you I would. I still will."

Mayhew said to the Wagon Hammer hand, "Go on."

"When Hand rode off," the rider continued, "the first thing we did was count. We missed Kenney. We built fires on the bank here." He pointed to a pile of blackened embers on the slope below them, and then to another thirty yards away. "We found him that way."

"Where was his horse?" Coe cut in.

"He kept his feet. We pulled him out at daylight. He's around here somewhere."

"Kenney couldn't have been much of a rider then," Coe observed dryly.

The Wagon Hammer rider didn't say anything.

"Who else was with you?" Mayhew asked.

"Three other hands," Petrie said. "They're back at the place if you want to talk to them."

"How did you find out about this, Loosh?" Honeywell asked.

"I rode over here to see if Hand had raided it, because we expected him to."

"You could walk, then?" Flood asked. "Because I picked you up and slung you across your saddle after hitting you. Do you remember that?"

"It must have been somebody else," Petrie said, smiling slightly, looking Flood over curiously.

Coe shouldered past Mayhew and walked slowly up to Petrie. "Will you tell the rest of it, Petrie—what Flood did for you, or have we got to go somewhere else for that?"

"I don't know what you're talking about," Petrie said evenly.

Then Coe hit him, hit him so hard in the face that there was an audible sound of gristle and knuckle against bone and teeth, and Petrie sprawled down the rise and turned over once and lay on his face in the mud. Mayhew stepped up and touched Coe's arm, while Honeywell brushed Breckenridge aside with a wave of his arm, so that the foreman was standing by the Wagon Hammer rider and neither of them could move past his big bulk.

"I don't love a liar," Coe said thickly.

"Go get him," Mayhew said to Breck. Then to Coe and Flood, he said, "Come on."

They mounted, leaving Breck and Petrie and the Wagon Hammer rider, and rode back to where the guns were lying. Mayhew dismounted first, and picked up the belts belonging to Coe and Flood. Instead of handing the belts to them, he stood still, pushed back his Stetson and looked up at Coe.

"Coe, you won't like what I've got to say, but I reckon it don't matter much."

Coe kept silent.

"I've got to arrest Hand."

"On Petrie's warrant?" Coe asked.

The sheriff nodded.

"That man was killed over on Brush Creek, on Bar Stirrup land, by Bar Stirrup riders trying to stop a stampede," Coe said evenly. "His horse was shot and he was tromped. If you'll take the trouble to ride over, I'll show you the place."

"Which won't be a lot different from this one, will it?" Mayhew asked gently. When Coe said no, it wouldn't, Mayhew said, "Look here, Coe. You and Flood and Hand will tell me one story. That's three of you. Petrie, Breckenridge, Tim and three others tell me another. That's six. But you both agree on one thing; Kenney is a Wagon Hammer rider and he's dead. Petrie never lied to me, you never lied to me and Hand never lied to me, but one of you is trying to do it now. I warned your outfit and I warned Petrie's too, that I'd put up with no bloodshed, but there's a man dead now. It seems you both agree that Bar Stirrup riders shot him."

"On Bar Stirrup land," Coe reminded him grimly.

"I've got six men of Petrie's to your three that says it wasn't," Mayhew said patiently. "That's what I'll have to work on."

"And if I get a dozen men—the only men that could possibly ride for Hand—to tell you they didn't raid this herd, what then?"

"I could go over and find the same number of Wagon Hammer riders that said they did."

Flood saw Coe's jaw set and he knew that Coe was through talking, and that the name of Margot Curtin, the only person who could right this, would not be brought up. And then, if he had not before, Flood knew he had made no mistake about Coe.

"The trouble with you, Coe—you and every other man in this war, is that you don't think anybody is serious about it but yourself. Hand thought I was bluffing. He'll find I wasn't," Mayhew said.

"You haven't got him yet," Coe said.

"That's where you're wrong. I have. Hand is sitting at his own table with two of my men guarding him, while I'm out here getting what proof I can. That's the least I can do." He looked at them both now. "You can have these guns if you give me your word you won't try to free him."

"You can't have my word," Coe said.

"Nor mine," Flood said.

"I thought that was the way it would be," Mayhew said. He hung the two belts on the horn of Honeywell's saddle. "Maybe you better ride back to the place with us."

CHAPTER TEN

AT THE BAR STIRRUP, they found things as the sheriff had described them. Two temporary deputies were seated in the big room, rifles across their knees. Hand had ridden back from the Brush Creek camp and found them waiting for him. He had been allowed to cook up a meal, and the dishes were still on the table.

Hand looked at Flood and Coe as they entered ahead of the sheriff, and noticed immediately that they wore no guns, which was a sign he interpreted correctly.

"You still believe it then," Hand said to Mayhew.

"I've got to," the sheriff said. "You better come along with us, Ben."

"I'd like to talk to my men first."

"Go ahead," Mayhew said. Then he turned to one of the deputies. "Frank, get a tow-sack and load all them guns in it." He indicated the wall rack, which held the Bar Stirrup's modest armory. When it was done, Flood and Coe sat down on either side of Hand at the long table, while the sheriff stood in the door, out of hearing.

Coe said, "It was too slick, Ben. If I hadn't been at the line camp last night, I would have believed it myself."

"We should have ridden back and got that dead man," Hand said calmly. "From now on, we bury their dead, besides our own." He spoke to Flood now. "Remember that, because you are giving orders while I'm gone."

Flood shook his head. "Men will fight for you where they won't for me. They'll fight for Coe, too."

"You are working for me and taking my orders," Hand said slowly. "If you won't, get out."

Flood did not smile. "I'll stay."

"There's nothing more I can tell you," Hand continued. "Petrie will strike and he'll strike quick, before I have a chance to get out of jail."

"That will be soon," Coe said grimly.

"Take all the men you can get and scatter our stuff in the hills," Hand continued.

Mayhew walked across the room and Hand ceased talking.

"That's all the time I can give you, Ben. If your men ride in here now, there will be a fight."

Hand rose and walked unconcernedly to the door, without a back glance at Coe or Flood.

Mayhew spoke to them now. "I'm taking all the guns in the place, yours included. I'll dump the sack by the road in sight of town."

"That is more of the same kind of justice, Max," Coe said bluntly. "It leaves us in fine shape to welcome a gang of Wagon Hammer riders."

"Then you'd better take to the timber until you can get armed again," Mayhew advised. At the door he said, "Don't follow us."

Coe watched them ride off across the pasture and over the bridge, the hoofs of their horses beating an erratic thunder that wakened the valley. Then it died, leaving the sunny afternoon more still than ever. Coe's jaw muscles were corded, his face dark with anger, but he only said quietly, "Give them a few minutes' start."

He turned and went back to the cook-shed and in a moment returned with two opened cans of tomatoes, one of which he gave Flood along with a spoon.

They ate quickly, the look of leashed fury in Coe's face unchanging. He set his spoon on the table, and said, "Have you anything here you want to keep?"

"From what?" Flood said.

"Fire."

"No."

"I have," Coe said. He stepped into the bunk-room and returned with several things wrapped in a slicker. "We might cache a case of shells out in the timber, too."

Flood said, "This can't be helped, can it?"

"I don't see how," Coe answered. "It's the kind of a thing Petrie would do first, because he understands that a man will fight for a place he calls home, and that it's harder to fight without it, even if home was only a hard bunk and a roof that kept off the rain."

He took some shells down. "It will make a nice fire, anyway," he said tonelessly. They took a case of shells apiece and carried them out into the timber, where they kicked dirt and pine needles over them.

Coe straightened up then and looked squarely at Flood. "Do you think this Curtin girl will dare tell Mayhew the truth of this thing?"

"I don't suppose she will, if she loves Petrie," Flood answered.

Coe looked out over the valley. "You try, anyway. See her. She's a good girl, by all accounts. You try."

Flood touched his arm. "I'll try," he said. "What about you? You aren't going with me. Is that it?"

"Not with you," Coe said. "I won't tell you where I'm going, because Ben needs you more than he does me—any of us."

"Look—" Flood began patiently, but Coe held up a hand.

"Let it ride," he said. "I know what I'm doing."

"Not murder," Flood said, seeing the anger beneath Coe's calm.

"No, not murder," Coe said. They walked down to the house together and Coe went to his horse and mounted. "If you get Ben out, tell him to look up Hartley first, and then come up to the Brush camp—if it's still there. I'll get word up to Emory to move the cattle clear up in the hills."

He rode south, knowing that Flood knew Emory and his riders would be north and west. It was a gesture of simple and complete confidence in Flood, and there was no deceit in it. A distrustful man or even a cautious one would not have spoken as Coe did, and he would have ridden north out of Flood's sight in a careful attempt to disguise what he was about. Flood understood that a man cannot always reckon with his own anger, but while Coe's actions were those of an angry man, they were not those of an impulsive one.

He walked over to the corral and let the half dozen

saddle horses out, then came back and shut the house door and left on the Clear Creek road.

He met one rider on the way, and immediately pulled off the road into the timber on the off-chance that Petrie was a more careful man than he seemed.

When he found the tow-sack at the side of the road on the hill above town, he dismounted and strapped on his own gun. The rest he cached in the fork of a tree off the road.

The town had a different air about it today. There were a few buckboards and saddle horses at the hitchracks, and women were on the street.

Instead of hitching his horse in front of the hotel, Flood took him to the feed stable, and asked to have him grained and rubbed down.

He did not even glance at the marshal's office, but he felt that he was being watched. Now he remembered the door at the back of that small office, and he was certain that it let on to the jail where Hand would be. He would find out later.

In the hotel, young Curtin was behind the desk. At first, Flood thought that he had succumbed to the hot, drowsy late afternoon and was sleeping, but when he stepped to the desk, he saw Curtin put down a book.

"I'd like to see your sister," Flood said.

"She's not here."

"Where is she?" Flood asked.

Curtin rose out of his chair. Flood saw his face set in an expression of stubborn defiance.

"I don't consider that any of your damned business," Curtin said.

Flood said patiently, "Wouldn't it be easier to let me see her? I will, anyway."

"Not if I can help it," Curtin said grimly.

"I suppose she's asleep, isn't she?"

Flood saw his upper arm move a little, and guessed he was reaching for a gun below the counter. So when Curtin pulled the gun out, Flood was not surprised. But he did look at the gun. It was a heavy, single-action .45 caliber Colt, with an eight-inch barrel, and was new.

It takes a spread of hand to grasp a gun and bring a thumb up to flick back a stiff hammer; it takes a knowledge of how to handle a gun, too. Curtin had neither, and he was excited. Flood put a big hand out, put it swiftly, because Curtin was still trying to cock the gun with his small hand. Flood's full fist settled about the chamber and his thumb slid down into the slot where the hammer fell. He pulled easily and the hammer stabbed his thumb, and Curtin yanked the gun hard, then let go.

Flood laid the gun on the counter.

"You can go with me," he said. "I don't want to harm her."

"No, damn you," Curtin said sharply.

Flood was quiet a moment, musing. "I could break into every room, but that might cause trouble. You wouldn't want that." When Curtin said nothing, Flood added, "You see, I have to see her."

"What do you want with her?"

"If you will take me to her, I will tell you along with her."

Where the very unhaste in Flood's voice and manner might have angered another man, it made Curtin see the absurdity of his stubbornness, and yet there was a pride in him that would not admit it.

So Flood said, "I know. You have no cause to think well of me, and you want to protect her. But I have to see her."

And in saying it, Flood was assuming Curtin could protect her, so that the young man flushed a little, maybe with pleasure, and said, "But she's asleep."

"I thought she would be. If it wasn't important, I wouldn't want you to wake her."

"All right," Curtin said. He walked from behind the counter down the hall that ran beside the stairs. Flood followed him slowly. He saw Curtin softly open the second door, then step inside the room. A minute passed before Curtin swung the door open and bid him enter.

Margot had on a loose gray flannel wrap and she was standing beside the mussed bed. Her hair was still disturbed, and Flood noted it, liking her for not bothering to tidy it.

"What is it? Trouble?" she asked, in that warm impersonal voice that was slow with sleep.

"I have come to collect a debt," Flood said.

"Sit down." She said to her brother, "Will you lift the shade a little, Lee?"

The room had a warm yellow glow of sun through the window shades. The lifting shade let in a shaft of sunlight that leaped across the floor to Flood's feet. He was standing with his hat held in both hands before him, and he sat down on the nearest chair at her bidding.

Curtin leaned against the heavy old dresser.

"A debt, you say," Margot said. "I don't recall your ever doing anything for me."

"Maybe I was told wrong. I thought you were going to marry Petrie."

He could see her flush, could see a light of protest leap up into her eyes, but Flood knew that if there was ever a time to trade on his favor of last night, this was the time. His face did not change.

"Yes."

"Ben Hand is in jail," Flood said. "Petrie swore out a warrant for murder against him early this morning."

"How does that concern me?"

"It doesn't, except that you are the only witness Mayhew will believe to the fact that the man was killed in the Brush Creek stampede. Petrie had the body packed over to Silver Creek, then he and six of his riders swore that Hand stampeded a Wagon Hammer herd into that Silver Creek bog. He told Mayhew the man was killed that way. Mayhew believes him."

Margot was silent a moment, her face immobile. "Are you certain of that?"

"I was there when he said it," Flood answered. "Hand is in jail now."

"And who did kill this man?" Margot asked coldly.

"I think I did," Flood said calmly. "He was riding point, trying to swing the herd over. So was I. He shot at me, and I shot at him. His horse went down, and he was trampled."

"Then why are you asking me to free Hand since you ride for him?"

Flood leaned forward a little. "I am asking you to tell the truth. I want you to tell Mayhew that. Then let him judge if Hand is to be held."

"And you will tell Mayhew it was you that shot Kenney?"

"I haven't been able to get him to believe that I did yet," Flood said.

Margot stood up and walked over to the window. The sun turned her hair into stilled flame and where it caught the folds in the robe, made it seem white. She half turned to Flood.

"For a transient gunman, you bring honor up in queer places."

Flood didn't say anything. Curtin was looking from his sister to Flood, and Flood knew that she had told him of last night's happenings. He had the wisdom to see this was something only for his sister, and he kept silent.

Margot turned and walked slowly back across the room and sat on the bed, turning her head so she could study the wall. Finally she looked at Flood.

"Have you any idea what you have asked me to do?"

Flood nodded without saying anything.

"And does it please you?"

Flood lifted his hat from his knee and put it down again, feeling anger well up in him.

"I am not forcing you," he said.

"No."

"And I did not choose the man you are to marry, nor guarantee what he would do at a time like this."

Flood saw her wince, and he went on, "And there are other ways of settling this besides asking for your help. Whatever gunmen you seem to think I have behind me will not ride up and horsewhip you for telling me to settle this without you."

"I made a mistake that day. I—I have never seen you

again to apologize for it—except last night."

"The name might have led you to do it," Flood said, without any forgiveness or condemnation.

Margot stood up suddenly. "I had one part of it thought out last night," she said wearily. "The part about Loosh. I can even say that it was his shooting at you that did it." And now she turned on Flood. "But damn you! Why does it have to be you—a hired killer—that shows me all my mistakes?"

She was sobbing now, and walked over to her brother and buried her face in his shoulder. Her brother let her cry it out. Presently she quieted and said to Flood without turning, "If you'll leave, I'll dress and go with you."

In the lobby, Flood sat down and took out his pipe. He told himself that it was the inevitable course of events that had come between this girl and Petrie, not himself. Yet, as she had said so bitterly, it had come through him. He had come here to do what loyalty and justice demanded, hoping, hardly believing, that he could make a woman turn against the man she loved. And now that he had, he was almost shamed by it.

When she came out, dressed in a gabardine skirt, loose white blouse and boots, Flood put his pipe away and came over to her.

"There is one thing I will promise you," he said. "I will never let you suffer for having done this."

"That promise is a little too Olympian, even for you," she replied. "Shall we go?"

"Not yet," he said, standing still. "Not until you believe that."

"I would like to, but I can't. I—I know Loosh. He has already said he will kill you."

Flood saw the fear in her eyes, and for a moment he was appalled at what he had asked this girl to do. He only said, "Many men have said that."

"I know. I don't doubt your courage. But this is war, where courage doesn't count—only men, and the number of them."

"And I have survived wars too, to be able to make that promise," Flood said.

Clearcreek was set so deep in the hills that darkness came quickly. It was already dusk on the street when Flood and Margot left the hotel. Flood was a half head the taller, but her stride was a man's. He looked at her once as they walked toward the marshal's office, noting her straight back, the clean soft lines of her neck and jaw-line. He saw her face too, set and deadened, and he wished that Coe had come in his place.

The sheriff was at his desk, and for a moment after they entered, he did not look up from the papers before him, or speak. When he saw them, he looked first at Margot and rose, and then at Flood, and into his shrewd old eyes came a look of cautious wonder.

"Sit down, Margot," he said, indicating his chair.

"I have come to get Hand," Flood said.

"You can always try," Mayhew said. "What is it now?"

"If I prove to you that Petrie lied, that Kenney was killed on Bar Stirrup range trying to run off Bar Stirrup cattle, then your case against Hand will not hold, will it, Sheriff?"

"If you could prove all that, I reckon you would have this morning," Mayhew said slowly.

"I had the only proof," Margot said quickly. "Would you believe me against the word of Loosh and Breck?"

The Sheriff immediately said, "Yes."

"Then it happened as Flood told you," Margot said dully. "Loosh ran that herd on Silver Creek as bait, hoping Hand would strike there. He was so sure of Hand that he intended to stampede Hand's herds that same night up by the Bar Stirrup Brush Creek line camp. Hand outguessed him, and had men up there. When the stampede started he—"

"Wait," Mayhew cut in. "Were you there?"

"Yes."

"Why?"

Margot looked up at Flood, and then said, "You know Loosh, Sheriff. It—it was the way he did things."

"Bragging, you mean."

"Yes. In front of me."

She went on. "The biggest part of the herd was bedded down close to the salt lick. Loosh intended to swing them over the ridge to the east and down that steep slope into the creek gully. Hand's men saw that. He put men on the other side of the herd to hold them from turning. There—there was fighting. Kenney was hit and trampled in the stampede."

"Who shot him?"

"I did," Flood said quietly. "I was the rider trying to swing the lead steers around. He shot at me, and I hit him. I heard him go down, and all the rest."

In the following silence, Flood heard a man swing on to the walk outside, breathing heavily. He turned just as Honeywell stepped through the door.

"It's come, Max," the marshal said mildly. "Petrie is in town with a bunch of Wagon Hammer riders."

Flood's gaze shuttled to Margot. Her face had gone white. He could see that much in the dusk. Mayhew turned to the wall gun-rack and took down a rifle which he handed to Honeywell without a word. The big marshal looked at Flood, and said, "I wouldn't light that lamp, Max." He went out on the steps.

"Are you trying to get yourself in this jail or get Hand out?" Mayhew asked Flood.

"I have never heard of a man being arrested for killing a rustler unless he crossed a crooked lawman," Flood said.

Mayhew straightened up a little, and then exhaled his breath slowly, but it could be heard above the chattering clop of many horses' hoofs in the dusty street outside.

"I reckon I deserved that too," Mayhew said mildly.

"Yes," Flood said.

He heard a change in the sound from the street, and then it died altogether.

Petrie's voice came out of the dusk.

"Sam, is Margot in there?"

"Uh-huh," Honeywell said lazily.

"Is Flood with her?"

"Stay on that horse, Loosh," Honeywell said warningly.

"Tell him to step out here."

Mayhew walked over to Flood and took his gun out, and laid it on the desk. Then he waited.

Flood turned slowly, feeling his stomach ball up hot and hard within him, and walked to the door, just as Honeywell said, "He hasn't got a gun, Loosh. I have. Remember that."

The Wagon Hammer riders were grouped in the street in a loose half circle behind Petrie. The buildings across the way were lighting up against the darkening evening.

Flood stood beside Honeywell in the door. "Yes," he called.

Petrie said across the silence, clearly, with studied insolence, "That wench will sell you out the next turn, Flood."

Flood took two steps forward, and swung under the hitch-rack. Honeywell's gun eased to his shoulder.

Flood stopped. "Get off that horse."

"Stay in that saddle, Loosh," Honeywell said sharply.

Petrie's face raised a little. His hands met at his waist, hesitated, and his gun belt slid down, clicked when the gun touched his spur and clopped into the dust.

"You go to hell, Sam," Petrie said calmly. He swung out of the saddle and was already walking toward Flood when he touched the ground. Honeywell swung under the hitch-rack, his shotgun waist-high.

Petrie came close to Flood and stopped.

"I will not hear any man name her that—not even a sick man," Flood said to him.

Petrie struck out on Flood's last word, struck viciously, with the full throw of his corded shoulder muscles and body behind it. It caught Flood full in the mouth, instantly numbing all feeling there, slogging darkness into his brain, rocketing him back off his heels into the air. Something rammed into his back all across his shoulders, and then he heard a crash as the hitch-rail split and he fell his length across the sidewalk.

He dragged himself to his feet, holding his breath against the pain, and walked toward Petrie.

"This is not of my making," he said quietly through thickening lips, and kept on. Petrie's second blow he took rolling in and felt the electric lust as he returned a hooked forearm and it smashed into giving flesh. They were leaning shoulder to shoulder now, and Flood pumped all the power of his rage into those close blows that lifted Petrie back each time. When they broke away, Flood stumbled forward a little and his skull seemed set back on his shoulders by Petrie's savage lacing blows, three in thought-quick succession, all in his face.

It was Flood's dogged, senseless advance that Petrie could not fight off; nor could he escape the hot agony of his ribs being crushed with the regularity of dripping water as Flood's thick, slogging fists tore through his guard and smashed wind and blood and almost life out of him.

They had circled the motionless Honeywell now, so that Petrie's back was to the hitch-rack. He sensed this as soon as Flood did and stood his ground, the toes of his boots clawing into the dust.

And Flood went on. This time dodging or taking Petrie's aimed and grunting blows on the top of his head, his shuffling, widespread legs taking him into that circle of torment and through it, so that he was close to Petrie again, and could hear the slow suck of his breath as he fought to get more in his lungs. And he drove and lifted at the same time with his right hand and hooked in with his left arm crooked, with all his falling weight on it, and Petrie suddenly vanished before him.

Flood fell on his knee, looking, seeing Petrie's back on the hitch-rail, the axis for his body as the shock of those blows rocketed him away and higher until he writhed and kicked while the rail cracked and he fell entirely over it, his back arched in frozen protest.

Flood was crawling under the rail as Petrie lit on his side, his effort to rise instantaneous but the reaction of his muscles slow. They rose together, facing each other, only Flood rose with a gathering explosive power, his hands fisted while in the dust. And this time he did not aim at Petrie's body, but at the jut of his chin and when he drove it through Petrie's unready guard to connect he knew it was over.

He followed it through, so that his arm was deep across his body as Petrie hurtled into and through the glass window of the store. Flood heard the bell clear crash of the glass, even the hollow thud of Petrie's head as it hit the flimsy floor of the mean show window.

Petrie did not move, except that his head turned until it rested on his cheek as he lay there peacefully on his back, hands at his side. There were a few shards of glass on his chest, so suddenly and completely had he been stilled. His legs from the knees down hung out into the street, heels almost touching the walk.

Flood could not smother the wild panting that heaved his whole upper body, and when he tried to lift an arm to wipe the blood from his face, he knew he would have to wait until strength returned.

He heard Honeywell say in his sad certain voice into the silence, "Drift along, Wagon Hammer. We'll bring him over to the Palace."

Flood teetered around on a heel to face them, trying to still his breathing. These men were still in the loose half circle, their tensed bodies only black silhouettes against the light from the other side of the street.

Margot came out of the office to Flood's side and took his hand. Mayhew stepped out after her, a shotgun sagging in the crook of his arm.

It was Breck who said from among the horsemen, "Flood, Hand will never leave that jail alive."

Mayhew's voice whipped out over the stillness and there was no tolerance in it this time.

"Breck, unless you move them men there's goin' to be legal murder here."

Breck made the first reluctant move, and all the other horses seemed to move with his.

Margot said simply to Flood, "That was a decent thing, Mark."

He looked into her eyes and they held a hope he had never seen in them before.

"I promised you," he said.

Then he watched the light die in her eyes, but she did not take her hand from his.

"I'd like a handkerchief—and my gun," he said.

Honeywell was still standing in the street, his vast and shapeless bulk turned doggedly toward the dispersing riders, but Mayhew walked over to Flood.

"A man never deserved that more," he said quietly to Flood. "Now take her home. I'll turn Ben out when it's safe to."

He handed Flood his gun and Flood holstered it, sick with weariness.

As he turned, Honeywell called slowly from the street, "I liked that, Flood."

They walked in silence, Flood's heels dragging on the board walk without his knowing it. People they passed on the street went about their business, some looking at Flood with friendly curiosity. At the door of the hotel, Margot said, "You look terrible. Come in and wash up."

"Hand is not free yet," Flood answered, and then he said what he had been wondering this past minute. "You will not find it easy here now, will you?"

"No," Margot said dully.

"Have you no other place to go?"

"No." She put a hand on Flood's arm and smiled at him. "You see, I made my choice long ago, Mark."

Flood said, "He cannot and will not hold you to that."

"He was angry and hurt," Margot said, but without any spirit. "If he has always treated me well, then the least I can do is to not side in with his enemies."

"Yes," Flood said. "But I made a promise, too. I will keep that."

"You have already."

"But this is not over," Flood insisted.

"I'm afraid it is for you, Mark," Margot said. "I fore-saw all this when you came to me, yet I had to go through with it. It would be better if you left me to settle it my own way." She turned, smiling at him. "Thank you for trying to put right what was wrong from the beginning."

And Flood watched her go, a bitterness in him that he could not smother.

CHAPTER ELEVEN

WHEN COE LEFT FLOOD and rode south, there was a rage in him that seemed as if it had always been there and would never die. He had felt it once before. That time he had killed a man, and ridden away; and he had never regretted it. But what he was about to do now he knew he would regret. No, he would regret not so much what he was about to do as the way he went about doing it. But there is a time for all things, he reflected, knowing there wasn't but not caring. The image of that lying, plotting Petrie rose before him, and then the picture of Ben Hand, the man he loved, crowded it out of his mind. He saw Hand in jail, helpless, chained by a lie, and the injustice of it was hot in his blood.

He stopped first at a mean cabin and talked without dismounting, after refusing politely to eat. The man he talked to was in bib overalls, a faded, dirty man who kept kicking a yapping cur away from Coe's horse. It ended with the man coming with him. His second stop was at a similar place, and here he met with refusal from a white-haired man who kept shaking his head all the time Coe talked. But at the third, fourth and fifth places—some better than others—were men who listened to him and came with him. Some places he picked up two and three men.

And then he swung over to the small ranches and tried them, and men came with him. These men were grim-faced, and they looked on the first recruits with ill-concealed contempt. But they came. So did others, whom he summoned by sending out his first recruits, so that it was still early afternoon when the crowd of them rode up to a small shack deep into the Wagon Hammer range.

"I don't have to go over all this again," Coe told them. "This is your chance to down him. God knows, he has given enough cause." He paused. "Or has he?"

They nodded or yelled or merely said yes as their feelings prompted them. Coe hated nearly all their faces, their mean small spirit as reflected in their mob bravery, and he hated himself more. But he had to admit he had chosen well. Every man of them had a real or fancied grievance against Petrie and his Wagon Hammer outfit. Most of them were squatters, whom Petrie moved out at will, as does any big outfit plagued by their whining and their borrowing and their stealing. Others were small ranchers whom Petrie had antagonized or frozen out or overrun or just bullied. Coe had put them a blunt proposition. With their help, Petrie would be ruined by morning. Would they risk a neck to see it done? It seemed they would.

He went on. "There won't be more than a half dozen men riding herd, but those men must not be allowed to get free. Understand that?"

They did, it seemed, and with much grinning.

"I don't want you to comb that range for every head, but get most of them—far more than half. It will be easy because most of the Wagon Hammer stuff has been thrown down in this corner for loose herding. Line out and take it fast, and don't beat the brush. You'll get enough without it, and we can't spare the time. Try to be at Alamoscita Springs by dark."

One man said, "It's a hell of a waste of good beef, it seems like, Coe."

"If you kept what you found, they'd be building a new jail in Clearcreek," Coe said bluntly. It seemed they agreed on that too.

Another man said, "Only one thing ain't so good

about this, Coe. What's he goin' to do?"

"I've told you he's got a war on his hands that will keep him busy. If this goes through, he won't have the money to pay fighting men, and without men, he can't do any more to you than I could alone. Besides that, I doubt if he'll win this fight."

When they received fuller instructions, they rode off. Coe counted over forty men. A sober-faced rancher pulled up beside Coe and watched them go.

"That's a hell of a crew to let write their own ticket, Coe," he said grimly. "They'll kill and barbecue every Wagon Hammer rider."

"Can you think of another way?" Coe asked grimly.

"No. I don't even like to think of this."

"Nor do I." He looked over at the man. "Do you want to pull out, Yancey?"

The rancher shook his head. "No. I've waited years to see it done. Why did they come now when you called them?"

"Didn't you ever see a dog fight?" Coe asked softly. "They all pile on the down dog. They think Petrie's down—or will be. And so he will."

Four different times that afternoon Coe heard gunfire. He tried to forget those times in work, in directing his end of this sweep. It was haphazard, but the open, rolling country stippled with clusters of trees and free of deep ravines or canyons made it easy. Petrie had thrown his herds down in this far corner of his range away from where he reckoned the fight would be. Coe had guessed long since that he would, and had known it when he rode over the Wagon Hammer range the week before and saw it almost cleared of cattle. It was a fool thing for Petrie to do, but his arrogance had made him underestimate Hand's ability. A few quick forays a little way into the Wagon Hammer range was all Petrie gave Hand credit for being able to swing. And if his herds were out of the way, even those would be fruitless. As for the dozen mean nesters squatting on the fringe of his domain, Petrie had never given them a thought. Mice do not attack a fox. And yet they would,

Coe reflected; and they would do it with a vindictiveness that left nothing to be wanted.

As far as sight went, he could see men pushing bunches of a dozen or so cattle into the herd which was pooled now down in the shallow valley before him. There must be four or five hundred there, and over to the south and north, there would be six or eight more herds like it.

Riders kept moving this herd down the valley toward the springs, and picking up more cattle on the way which were pushed into the main stream. It was fat beef, neither thirsty nor hungry, and docile, so it moved at a good pace. Coe kept watching the sun, wishing that in some way he could blot it out and have night for a cover. Three hours ago, he had been praying for more daylight, but now he saw he would have enough and to spare.

But it was deep dusk, almost night, when they reached the springs. There was still enough light for him to see the vast herd here on the flats beside the creek. And then, for some unaccountable reason, he thought of Flood and he knew that Flood would never have done this, nor let it happen.

For Flood was a man Coe liked and knew, although they had spent precious few hours together. This crawling, furtive, rabble-rousing destructive war was a thing Flood would dread, just as Coe dreaded it. To put men and families and outfits against each other by wanton destruction and cunning was a thing Coe hated, for he was wise enough to see that it would have no end. But he reasoned hotly that he had not called the turn, and that Petrie wanted it that way or he would not have done what he did.

But for a minute there, sitting motionless on his horse as the sharp cries of the riders around and below him kept urging cattle into that vast, slowly milling pool, Coe's courage almost failed.

Then it was over, for he saw it was too late to turn back. The hardest job lay ahead. These sullen, excited fools mounted on poor horses and helpless before more than fifty head of cattle would have to put this herd on the move.

It was full dark when they had. Coe organized it like a trail drive, with two riders at point, the lead steers following them. There were plenty of men to ride swing on each side and keep the herd bunched and moving, while the most of them rode drag and prodded on the laggards. They went east, the friendly night about them, as dark and secret as their thoughts.

Coe reckoned he had close to five thousand head of cattle here, better than two-thirds of what Petrie claimed was his entire tally. Riding from group to group, he questioned them. Had they run across Wagon Hammer riders?

Yes, they had. It had been easy—and fun to give those cursed greedy bastards some of their own medicine. One trio of Wagon Hammer men had put up a fight, but they were smoked out and cut down. Coe learned there had been a line camp up at the head of a timbered valley over to the north and east.

"Did you burn it?" Coe asked, knowing they had.

"Sure. And everything that was in it," one man boasted, and laughed.

"They were dead, though," another man put in quietly.

Coe turned away, sick. By count, he had found there were at least eight Wagon Hammer men accounted for. Only one of them, surprised at the foot of a shallow box canyon, had been spared. He had been tied and thrown into the brush, and his horse hobbled.

As the night progressed, Coe became easier. Even if a man had got to Petrie with word of this, it would be slow work to follow them. The night was thick and moonless. They had a little better than five miles to go, and even now they had moved off Petrie's range and were crossing one to the east that would be relatively strange to Wagon Hammer riders.

But Coe found that long ago his patience had been exhausted. From an idea, a belief, he had nursed this cursed thing into something bigger than he could comprehend. Envy rode on stronger wings than he had guessed. And now, with five thousand steers strung out over three-quarters of a mile in the night, the thought of waiting longer was intolerable. He remembered that he had not smoked since mid-afternoon and he rolled a cigarette and then was afraid to light it, although he knew the sound of the cattle moving would carry farther than the smothered light of his match. He threw the cigarette away and cursed, and rode up ahead, knowing he could do nothing to hurry things, but wanting some release from this tension.

It was slow, slow, timed to the ponderous swing of the earth itself. Coe cut out a mile to the side and listened, and he could hear nothing but the night noises and the infinitesimal rumbling, which he might have imagined. Then, suddenly worried something had gone wrong in his absence, he rode madly back to the herd— and found that everything was the same. They had not moved, it seemed, all the time he was gone.

And yet he could see the progress. Riding wide of the herd so as not to startle them, he rode up to the man who was picking the trail.

"How much more?" he asked.

"Soon now," was all the man would say.

"But name it, man!" Coe said harshly.

"I don't know. I do know we're over the hump and on the long slope."

"Don't forget," Coe said. "When it's safe, send a man back and pull out of here. Don't shoot, whatever else you do."

And still nothing, nothing but the quiet incurious movement of the herd, the occasional, short bawling of protest, and the throb of the earth under him and the sound of it in his ears.

He rode past the swing riders and heard them mouthing a bawdy song that yet was gentle and rhythmical and told the cattle they were being herded by friends.

He was close to the men riding drag when it happened. A shot ripped the night and then from far behind the herd came a half dozen more. Coe rammed in his spurs and rode for the group close to him.

"Fight them off the sides before you run!" he shouted, and cursed with bitter, almost tearful impotence as he swung his horse around and started toward the herd. Racing now, he pulled out his gun and started to shoot and yell, edging closer to the rear of the startled herd. Then, from across the herd, came more shots from the swing riders, and shouts. Someone over there had sensed that a stampede must be bred.

And it was only a matter of seconds before the slow rumbling turned into a pounding, muttering rumble. Coe felt a hot surge of excitement run through him. They were in motion now, stampeded by the racketing gunfire behind them, and what was more important, they were headed right. If he could make the lead, he could do it, and all the Wagon Hammer men in the country could not stop it.

He rode wildly, quirting his horse, not caring what happened to these men. Slowly but doggedly his horse was overtaking the herd, pushing toward the vanguard, while all to one side of him the panicky frantic bawling welled up to float above the thunder of the running cattle.

And now, as the width of the herd narrowed down to what he knew was the point of the dozen or so strong lead steers, he swung in toward them. A glance at the stars told him he was traveling east, the direction he must hold.

Then he roweled his horse until it stretched out in a dead run and he pulled up beside the lead steers, who did not swerve a foot from him in their wild, night-bred panic. He swung out ahead and his horse, goaded by the race and by fear too, took the lead. The nearest steer swung in dead behind him and Coe knew he had done it. The whole herd might spread out on a wide front, but they would hold this direction until they were forced and frightened off it or until they dropped from exhaustion.

Where the Wagon Hammer riders had made their blunder was in coming up from the rear. Now, nothing on earth could stem the mad, headlong rush of the herd.

Coe looked behind now, and could see nothing except the black line of cattle that faded into night behind him. Ahead was smooth gray sweep of grass, and nothing more, except the night and wind in his face.

How long? He did not know, but he swore that he would not leave this course until he did know, and swearing it, he felt sweat bead his forehead and his palms were wet.

But when he heard the first rock under his horse's feet he did know. This was the beginning of the rocky edge of the steep Barrier Rim. He pulled his horse sharply to the right and roweled him mercilessly. Looking ahead now, he could see where the gray line dropped off into the black of utter distance.

And then he looked to the other side, and heard before he saw. The herd had lined out on a wide front. He rose in his stirrups and cursed as he first made out the weaving dark line. His gun came up and he emptied it and still the line came.

So now he could see them and he settled back in his saddle. His horse would not turn into them, but shifted the other way, so that the blind blundering wave when it struck did not roll over him, but took him with them.

He felt the panic then, but only for a moment, for a short few yards. Then he heard the scrape and crunch of many, many hoofs bracing against a tide behind them that they could not stop.

He felt every muscle in his horse's back swell to bursting and then he floated forward, all knowledge fled and joined in the scream of his horse and the cattle, as he left the Barrier Rim for space.

He remembered dropping his gun.

CHAPTER TWELVE

STANDING IN FRONT OF THE HOTEL after Margot left him, Flood was aware of two things at once; the street was no place for him, and the blood on his face was caked like a mask of mud.

There was a clot of men close to the sheriff's office. Those would be the Wagon Hammer riders after Petrie. Flood crossed to the feed stable, walked down its wide center aisle and out to the horse trough in the corral at the rear. In the cool darkness, he stripped off his shirt and washed. The water bit into his raw knuckles, smarted his face and lips, and yet felt soothing. He sloshed it over his chest and back and felt his muscles gather a new strength in protest against its chill.

Finished, he paused in the rear door, where he could look through to the street. A half dozen saddle horses were in stalls, and he caught the sound of their rhythmical chewing and occasional stomping. He was ravenously hungry, yet he knew if he showed himself on the street now, there would be no place in this town he could finish a meal without trouble. When the Wagon Hammer men had Petrie with them and saw him and listened to Breck's bitter, vindictive tongue, they would hunt the town for him. Mayhew and Honeywell could police them just so long as they did not find him. Flood looked up into the dark hay-lofts that rose above the stalls on either side of the big centerway. Why not there?

He traveled down the long aisle toward the front, paused, then turned and climbed a stall and swung himself up to the overhang and was in deep hay.

Soon he had found a place against the front of the building where the weathered boards had parted enough to allow him a view of the street. He could see the hotel through one crack, and by moving five cracks down, he could see the sheriff's office too. It was still dark, and now the crowd in front of the shattered store window was gone. Something moved in the door of the sheriff's office and quieted again. That would be the sad marshal, guarding the jail.

Flood settled back into the soft hay and let weariness flow over him in a slowly pulsing wave. It was warm up here against the roof in the hay, and he wanted to sleep, but the knowledge of danger glowing like a coal in his mind would not let him drowse. He had seen lynchings and knew how they were made. A dozen sullen men drinking in a saloon, with their enemy in jail just across the street. Whisky and their own words would give them courage. A word, a look, a gesture would start it off into something only guns could quell.

Sometime soon, Morgan or Emory or Coe would ride in, and their entrance might kindle this flame. Hand had to be moved out of jail, and Flood wondered if he could not walk across the street, put a gun on Honeywell and then take the chance of bluffing it out beside Hand against those men watching from the Palace Saloon. He would do that if he had to.

He knew soon that he would have to smoke if he wanted to keep awake. He packed his pipe carefully, lighted it carefully and put out the match between his fingers. A spark in this hay would touch off an inferno, but now that seemed of secondary importance.

Toward the end of the second hour, he saw eight Wagon Hammer men cross the street to the hotel. Mayhew sauntered after them, a shotgun crooked in his arm. They did not stay long there, but crossed to the feed stable. Flood guessed that the stableman below had been watching this business, for these men stopped at the door and he was there to speak with them. Through the crack, Flood could see Mayhew leaning against a building across the street, and then he forgot him as Breck spoke below.

"You know him. Where is he?"

"I couldn't say. His horse is still here," the stableman replied. One of the men went back to look and confirmed this.

"I saw him come in here," Breck said.

"All right, look," the stableman said. "This place has two doors, remember."

"He likely walked through," one man said.

"We'll look, anyway," Breck said surlily. "Get up there in the loft."

"You take a lantern or light a match up there and you'll get run out of town," the stableman said grimly.

"And who will do it?" Breck asked.

"Not me. The sheriff, the marshal, and every man owning property in this town will do it. You start a fire in that hay and the whole town will go."

"All right," Breck said after a pause. "Get up without a light," he directed one of the riders.

The man swung up on the side opposite Flood. He beat around blindly in the hay, then called down: "I could be standing on him and wouldn't know it."

"Come on down," Breck said disgustedly. They walked down the center aisle and out the back and it was quiet again. But that was only on the surface. Flood heard Mayhew make his solitary way through the stable after them and go out the back. Honeywell still stood in the door of the office. Every twenty minutes, Honeywell would flare a match, and for the next five minutes there would be a glowing pinpoint of red in the door that did not move. Then it would arc out into the street, and the door would be dark again.

Flood watched it with a tension that grew within him. The town darkened a little as it grew later, but nothing else changed. He guessed it was close to midnight when a rider on a blown horse swung into the main street and galloped down it, his solitariness making his haste seem more urgent. Flood listened and guessed the man stopped at the Palace. It was only a matter of seconds before Flood heard men running on the board walk. In a moment, all the Wagon Hammer riders boiled past the stable and out of town. Petrie rode at their head.

Flood climbed down and crossed to the sheriff's office, which was lighted now. Honeywell greeted him sadly.

"What has the Bar Stirrup done now?"

"I wouldn't know," Flood said. "You had better let Hand out now."

"You don't figure that was a trick, then?"

"That horse that came in was close to spent when I saw him."

"All right," Honeywell said. "We'll wait for Max."

Mayhew stepped inside in a moment and opened the

rear door. Another one behind it, this of steel, had to be unlocked. Honeywell held the lamp while Mayhew went back into the tiny four-cell jail.

Hand squinted against the light as he stepped out into the corridor. Honeywell handed him his gun belt, and said, "You better clear out of here now. Your horse is over at the feed stable."

Hand said, "I didn't mind this so much, but I will not come here again."

Flood did not talk until they were clear of town, and then he told Hand all that had happened.

"You say this Curtin girl's word is what decided Max?"

"Yes."

Hand did not say anything for a time, and then he said, "I would never have believed it."

He asked about the fight with Petrie and said nothing about it when Flood finished telling him.

"Then you did not warn Emory like I told you," Hand said.

"Coe did."

"And where are they now?"

Flood told him he did not know.

"Then something has happened," Hand said.

Flood said it looked that way, for a Wagon Hammer rider had come into town on a high lonesome and taken Breck and all the other Wagon Hammer hands out with him.

"That means trouble," Hand said. He looked across at Flood in the dark. "I left you in charge, and still you cannot tell me what my own men have been doing."

Flood reined up and so did Hand. Flood said, "Hand, I will not run your fight. I tried to tell you that. You gave me two simple orders and then told me to run this as I liked. I did."

"If it is money you are after, I will pay you what I pay Emory and place you over him."

"I have never said I wanted either."

"Then what is it you want?"

"What I have now," Flood said. "But what I do not

want is to direct a man's own war for him. I will not do it."

Hand spurred his horse and Flood fell in beside him again. The night was quiet all about them, and only occasionally could Flood hear the muted hiss as the wind stirred the pines on either side of them. He knew now that it was too late for him to be classified as just another Bar Stirrup rider. Hand had never acted as if he were, and now he had said so. All the blessed anonymity that he had sought in this country was long vanished. He could not help being a figure in this quarrel after today even if he wanted to, and now he did not. But to shoulder the responsibility, to have to recall the consequences of what was happening and accuse himself of making them, he would not do.

Hand said quietly into the night, "Money will buy a man anything but his own destiny. I thought I could buy you to help me shape mine, Flood. I see I can't."

"You bought and paid for your own there in the Palace yesterday," Flood said. "Yes. A man can."

If Hand could find any reproof in that, he was welcome to it, Flood thought.

Hand said, "What was there left for me to do besides fight?"

Flood was not going to say that he should have forgotten his pride, for pride is too often bought with blood, and that is why it is so necessary. He was going to tell him that this quarrel was between Petrie and himself, and that somehow it should be made to remain that, yet when Flood thought of saying it, he knew he was suggesting the impossible.

"Every man settles that for himself," Flood said. "But if you are not careful, no man can live in peace in this country when you two are finished."

"You mean I should have forced a shoot-out."

"If it could have been done, yes."

Hand did not speak for a minute, and then he said in a voice strangled with anger, "I am not a coward, Flood."

"No man has said that," Flood answered mildly. "But

men are going to fight who do not hate each other. They will die because there was a piece of land in their country that Ben Hand wanted."

Hand said hotly, "Leave off, Flood! I have thought that enough without your saying it to me."

"Then don't try to bribe me to take your blame," Flood said.

"Why are you here?" Hand asked bluntly, swiftly.

Flood did not answer and Hand did not ask again. It was as if the question had gone unasked as well as unanswered. When they came to a fork in the road which Flood had noticed, he said, "Coe said to ride to Hartley. He will tell you what Coe is about."

"We'll ride home first," Hand said.

When, a few minutes later, the road tilted down through the trees and opened on to the edge of the valley across from the Bar Stirrup, they both saw the mound of glowing coals where the house had been. It showed plainly and almost pinkly against the night.

Flood heard Hand stir in his saddle.

"Did you know this had happened?" Hand asked quietly.

"Coe guessed it would. So did you, didn't you?"

"Yes."

Hand made no move to ride over to the burned cabin. It was as if he were struggling to put this behind him too. Presently he said in an almost peaceful voice, "I think that is a good sign. It means Emory fought them off at the line camp, so they could not get at the herd. He did this because there was nothing left to do."

He turned his horse up the valley and they had ridden a half mile almost into the sparse timber, when he added, "I think I will take my five men and fight him with them. I think I can. I would not like to see those men loyal to me get this too." He gestured back toward the burned house.

Flood wondered if those hours in jail had made Hand see things which he would not stop to consider before. He believed it had, and he was glad. The timber opened on to a large sloping prairie which they crossed going north-east. Picking up the road at its far side, they kept to it another mile until it forked into a cleared space where a cabin stood.

They were expected, for Emory stood in the door with a rifle and a lantern. His companion was a stooped, gaunt man with bitter eyes and gray hair. Hand introduced him as Hartley, and he shook hands with Flood, while Hand asked Emory, "What happened?"

"They came. Coe sent word up he thought they would, and we scattered our stuff into the high timber," Emory said.

"Was there a fight?"

"No. But when they went to round up the stuff, we kept worrying them with rifles. They gave up."

"Anybody hurt?"

"Morgan. They caught him in a coulee and rode him down. Killed him."

"Ah," Hand said. "And then they rode off?"

"Yes. The rest of us worked till dark shoving the cattle as high and as far as we could. Most of the stuff is close to timber line now."

Hartley said, "Get down and come in, Ben."

"Where is Morgan?"

"Up there," Emory said quietly. "Nosey is watching."

Hand dismounted, Flood following, and they entered the cabin. Emory said, "I waited until dark and then rode down. I found the place burned, but this Swanson kid Coe sent up to us told me to wait at Hartley's. I figured Flood was just about enough Bar Stirrup man to be in Clearcreek."

"You didn't," Hartley said grimly. "I did. I had to put a gun on him to keep him here."

The inside of the shack was neater than if a woman kept it. Hartley took down a skillet and threw in several steaks, while Hand told him and Emory what had gone on in Clearcreek. When he told of Flood's fight, Emory looked over at Flood with appraising eyes. The look Hartley gave him was a different one, one in which there was pity and some contempt. Flood reckoned Hartley an old friend of Hand's who had refused to take sides in this fight or have anything to do with it.

Hand was asking Emory now about Coe, but Emory could tell him no more than he knew.

"I thought he was with you until you rode up here," Emory said.

Flood thought of Coe as he had left him that morning, and then his mind shuttled to those Wagon Hammer riders who had left town in such haste. Somehow, Coe was connected with that, Flood was sure.

The food was ready and Flood and Hand ate, while Emory and Hartley watched. As soon as they were finished, Flood, Hand and Emory turned in, leaving Hartley to sit up for Coe.

Flood did not know what time it was when he was awakened by the scrape of Hartley's chair on the floor. He watched Hartley put out the light and go to the door and open it. In a moment, the older man stepped out into the night, and then returned to get the lantern and went out again.

Flood rose, and so did Hand, who had heard it too. Outside, they found Coe's friend of the bib overalls astride a horse which was nearly foundered. He had asked for Hand, and Hartley waited while Hand walked up beside him.

"Coe said to come to you," the man said.

"Where is he, Swanson?"

"Dead," Swanson said. "Leastways, I think he is." But in spite of the solemnity of the news he was bringing, he chuckled softly, looking at Hand. "Don't never say you ain't got friends in this country, Ben."

"What is it?"

"Close to five thousand head of Wagon Hammer cattle is piled up at the foot of the Barrier Rim," Swanson announced.

Hand said quietly, "What's that you say?"

"It's the truth. Coe come around to me about noon and told me his idea. It never took us long to get a bunch together. We made a quick drive down on the south pasture where most of Petrie's stuff was throwed together. Then we drove them across to the Rim. About a mile from it, them Wagon Hammer riders come down on us, but they come in from behind and started off a stampede. The last we seen of Coe, he was ridin' hell for leather to keep 'em headed right. Taken only a little while for 'em to get to the Rim and they piled over it to the last head." He chuckled reminiscently, then swore in slow humor. "If we'd of give that one Wagon Hammer hand what the others got instead of tyin' him up, we'd of got away clean. He broke loose and got word to Petrie. It don't matter much, though."

"What did the others get?" Hand asked, his speech beginning to thicken and betray his unbelief.

"I reckon you know that without my sayin'," Swanson answered.

For one fleeting poised moment, Hand looked at Flood, then a harsh savage sound welled up in his throat and he clawed at his gun. Flood leaped at him, his arms pinning his hands to his sides. Hand wrestled in speechless fury.

Flood said between clamped jaws, "Get gone, you fool!" to Swanson.

The man sat his horse for a surprised moment, then opened his mouth to speak, when Hartley stepped up and cut his horse a savage blow across the rump, and said, "Get out while you can, damn you!"

Swanson fought his startled horse, wheeled it and vanished out of the circle of lamplight, yelling illiterate curses over his shoulder.

Flood released Hand then, who stood looking off into the night. Then he turned and walked back into the house past Emory, who stepped out of the doorway to let him by.

Hartley came in and gently set the lantern on the table, and they all stood in the circle of its light, watching Hand.

Hand raised his head slowly, turning the bleak fury of his gaze on Flood.

"This is why you would not tell me where Coe was."

Flood looked from Hand to Emory, who was watching him with still, cold hate in his eyes. Only Hartley was not troubled, but he was watchful.

"You have made the name of Hand a curse," Hand said in slow, flat tones. "Those seven were not Wagon Hammer riders. They were friends helping Petrie out."

"I knew less about it than you did, Hand," Flood said, a warning edge to his voice. "Be careful of your talk."

"Seven men murdered because you wanted to win this fight your way."

"Even a fool can be just, Hand," Flood said narrowly. His eyes held smoldering pinpoints of anger. "Coe did not tell me or he would never have gone."

"I put you over him."

As Hand's vibrant voice fell and died, all of them heard a horse trot into the clearing outside and then stop.

"Mark Flood!" a voice called—Margot's voice.

Flood stood still a moment, then took a step. Hand raised his arm, barring Flood from the door. "Go see her," he said to Emory. Flood waited quietly, his eyes as steady as Hand's were hot.

Emory stepped out into the night and returned in a moment.

"She wants him alone."

"She can say what she has to say here," Hand said.

Flood said with ominous gentleness, "Hand, you or no man will tell me what to do."

With slow, solid steps he walked past Hand and out the door, and Hand watched him with murder in his face.

Outside Flood walked over to Margot, and she had already begun to speak as she dismounted. "Mark, you must go! Now! They are after you!"

"Who?"

"Mayhew. Something awful has happened! Petrie rode into town and woke up the sheriff. He swore out a warrant for you on charges of participating in the steal of that Munro herd—the one your brother was hanged for. He swore out a warrant against Hand for the murder of seven men!"

"Are you sure of this?" Flood asked. She was close to him now and some of the excitement in her voice was calmed.

"Yes. Honeywell came over and told me to warn you."

"Honeywell?" Flood echoed.

"Mark, don't you see they like you? They know you are not guilty. But it is all they can do—Mayhew can do, because something terrible has happened to Petrie. What is it?"

"I have got to tell Hand this," Flood said quietly.

"Of course. Honeywell expected that. But what has happened, Mark?"

"You will know soon," Flood said bitterly. "It will make this range a bloody hell." He could sense her, almost see her, close to him, and he could hear her breathing. "Margot, you should never have done this. Have you got to add this to what you will suffer from Petrie? Couldn't Lee have come with the word?"

"I pay my debts too, Mark," she said softly.

"But—I can't leave you," Flood said. "Because Petrie will find out and God knows what he will do to you."

"I knew you would say that," Margot said calmly. "Sam Honeywell has moved into the room behind mine, Mark. He said he would when I asked him, and I asked him because I knew you wouldn't leave without my being safe. I will be."

"Yes, Honeywell is a man to trust. But still it was foolish."

"You haven't much time, Mark," Margot said softly. "Do you think I could let you ride out without showing that I am grateful? This is my way, Mark."

Flood grasped her tightly by her shoulders. "I've broken into your life enough, Margot," he said quietly. "You saved an innocent man from jail because I asked you to, and not until I fought with Petrie did I know what I had done. You are afraid of him—but there is an understanding between you, an understanding I have no right to question. Yet fearing him, you ride out to me now. If he discovers it, I will have come between you forever."

"What if I want you to, Mark?" Margot asked softly.

Slowly, Flood's hands dropped to his side. "You don't know what you are saying."

"Loosh Petrie is nothing to me now, Mark," Margot said steadily. "Last night when he shot at you, and when he cursed me this afternoon, I knew it was finished. I only wanted a way to break it off, a way that would not drag you into it. But should I think of that when you are in real danger?"

Flood said, "I am a stranger to you. I would not do that much for a stranger myself."

"I was a stranger to you, Mark, and you did more than this for me. Where is the difference?"

"I will tell you," Flood said, his voice low and urgent. "You are fresh and honest, sure of yourself and your life. I rode in here to hire my guns, and my dirty job made me ask you to help the man that pays me. You did not even owe it to me to be fair, because what I asked you to do was unfair. And now, because of me, you're alone and afraid. Is that right?"

"Yes," Margot said quietly. "It is right because I was all wrong, and ready to make a mistake that I could never have wiped away. You did nothing, Mark, except have the courage to show me and tell me that the man I thought I loved did not even respect me." She paused and when Flood said nothing, she went on, "It's true I don't know you. But I do know that you could never do a dishonest thing in your life, could never hurt—"

Her talk stopped as Flood put a hand over her mouth. He waited a moment and took it away.

Margot smiled in the dark as he folded her to him and kissed her, and the fragrance of her hair and the feel of her parted, warm lips was like a drug rioting through him.

"Oh, Mark," she whispered.

Flood held her out before him, his eyes searching the dark for her face. "Margot," he said huskily, "I have no right to do this. Not because of Petrie. But—but I am not free."

"Then I will go with you, Mark!"

But before Flood's eyes rose the vision of those eleven men who had trusted him, and who were dead now, and he knew that if he turned from them, there would be no peace in his life from this moment on. A weary bitterness welled up in him and he could not stem it.

"It's not that," he said gently. "You don't know why I am here, Margot, and I cannot tell you. I will not make you share it. But I cannot come to you until it is done. If it were only running away from a warrant, I would not care. But I cannot run. I must stay here."

"But you must go, Mark, and I will go with you."

"No. I will go alone, but I will be back when all this is settled."

"But where will you go?"

Flood thought a moment. "There is a town across the mountains, I have heard. I believe I can get to it through that notch at the head of the Silver Creek range. I will go there."

"Alone," Margot said dully.

"And do you believe that I will be back, because I want you and because then I can speak as a man who is neither hunted nor hunting? Can you wait?"

"Yes," Margot said simply.

"Then go back to town," Flood said gently. "Sam Honeywell will watch out for you, and you must wait."

"Tell me one thing, Mark. Must you really go?"

"I could never have any peace if I turned back now," Flood said.

Margot kissed him again and clung to him hungrily for a few still seconds, then she broke away from him and turned to her horse.

"Mark, good-by, darling."

"Good-by," Flood said softly.

When her horse was lost in the black of the night, Flood stood motionless in the dark. Then he roused himself. He turned toward the cabin, walking, drawing his gun, so that Emory, who was standing in the door, drew back as Flood walked into the shaft of lantern light and stepped over the sill. He paused there, the gun firm in his hand, thinking how this was the second exit he had made this way.

"They are coming for you, Hand, and for me too. I believe our ways split here," he said.

"Yes," Hand said. "If I had thirty pieces of silver, I would pay you off as you should be paid."

"The charge is murder, Hand. Seven men," Flood said quietly, ignoring Hand's insult. "If you ever let them get you in jail, you are a hanged man."

"Some day, when this fight is bled out, Flood, I will come for you too."

"I can save you that. I will be back," Flood said. He stepped out the door. "Don't come out till you hear me ride off."

CHAPTER THIRTEEN

FLOOD RODE STRAIGHT FOR THE MOUNTAINS, and was deep in the Silver Creek range by sunup. He had wanted to leave this country as he would shed a coat, with no ties and no loyalties behind him. But thinking of Margot now, he knew that he was leaving it for only a while, and that as long as there was life in him he would ride back. His mind was full of her, and he could hear her warm voice and feel her body against him until the longing for her was an ache inside him. He knew he had not been fair to her, that he should not have spoken until this mission was behind him and done with; but it deepened his resolve to go through with this. She had understood him, because she understood a man's silence and a man's honor, and with that he was content.

He reflected too, that in the course of a few days, he had ridden the crest of a bloody and violent wave that was only now receding for him. And from all those hours, those hired loyalties, he had emerged with her—and with the brief bright memory of Coe. He thought of Ben Hand with the impersonal pity he might have had for a cornered animal. Hand was a man who bred strange loyalties, but he was also a man who could not understand the depth of them. Poor, gallant, unwise Coe had in one night rocketed a quarrel between two men into a fight that might well rage for years. And Ben Hand, the man who had won that devotion, did not understand it, could see none of the fineness in it.

When Flood reached the very point of the range where it tilted up into the rocks, he paused and looked behind him. A range worth fighting for, hadn't Coe said? And a range now that would be bought with the blood of too many men.

And thinking this, Flood remembered that he had a share in this range too, and that his share had been paid for by Shifflin and those nine men who had vanished here. For Flood believed still that one of the men fighting for this Silver Creek range knew the fate of Shifflin's men. If the next two days proved that there was a way through these mountains to a town on the other slope, then he would be sure of it, and he would know too where the Shifflin herd had gone.

He looked up through the sparse timber to the rocky slope before him. He had little to go on, except Coe's word that a town lay beyond, but perhaps over there was the certainty that would lift this range war beyond a fight for long and give it a meaning for him.

As he threaded his way through these high rocks and boulders, he could see that cattle had been up this far. It might mean that they had strayed from the lower range, but as he rode deeper into the notch and the signs continued, he was certain that these were not the signs of strays.

He marshaled all he knew of these men below with whom he had lived and fought. Putting away his loyalties and prejudices, he tried to be just to them. When he thought of Petrie, he discounted the fight, and tried to remember that a man who will misname a woman sometimes has a strange sense of honor concerning stealing. But what he could not forget was that Petrie was a liar, and that he had framed Hand with a primitive cunning. He thought too of Petrie's arrogance, his craftiness, his daring, and he concluded that Petrie's name bulked large with guilt. He could conceive of stealing a trail herd, and he had what was needed to carry it off.

Then he thought of Hand, as he looked about him at the hard, gaunted mountain land that towered above and on all sides of him. If this was the trail of the stolen herd, then he was certain that Hand could never have conceived of this way, because it took a kind of daring and imagination that Hand did not possess. If either Petrie or Hand were fighting for Silver Creek for the right of way to this pass, then it was Petrie who wanted it. He wanted it because he was the thief of Shifflin's trail herd—and of the Munro herd too, probably. But Flood knew how useless this guessing was, and that a hunch is a coin unnegotiable in a court of law. Proof was what he needed, and proof was what he must have.

And that settled in his own mind, he forgot it. He was following a faint trail now around the shoulders of mountains that blanketed distance with their vast bulk. Since sunrise he had been climbing and now he was close to white fields of snow. Occasional warped and stunted conifers found a hold between the rocks. A hardy grass Flood had never seen before battled with them for the little soil in the desert of rock.

Sharp winds raced along every canyon and swept Flood with the clean cold of the stars. By noon, he was lost in this profound upland labyrinth of rock and great slashed canyons that twisted and fell, and tumbled and angled and doubled back, and never escaped from the penning peaks. He had only one thing to guide him, and that was the trail that daily rains had beaten and smoothed and blotted out. But there were signs, such as the rare fields of soft rock that the feet of many cattle had almost pulverized, leaving a clear trail.

Too, when this trail narrowed, and where cattle had been hazed into a tight defile, there were tufts of hair wedged in the cracks of the irregular wall where cattle had milled and pushed to hurry their turn.

And once, where the shaley trail threaded the edge of a deep canyon, Flood saw far below the carcass of a steer. He dismounted and climbed down to the bottom of the dank canyon. It was narrow, and a tiny stream of snow water cut its floor. The steer lay across the stream, a little bloated. On the left hip, which was uppermost, Flood saw where a generous square of hide had been cut out, and all the brands with it.

The very fact that someone had taken the precaution to do this indicated to Flood that a herd had been driven through here in secret. He squatted on his heels, shivering with the cold, his pulse quickened by this new evidence. Then, on the chance that these brand blotters had missed something, he felt the stiff ears of the steer for a hidden earmark. There was none. They had been careful.

As if they knew that even though nobody would come along at this exact spot and look down here and even come down here, all that was no excuse for taking chances, he thought. He admired their doing it, but he also knew that anyone so careful would have his trail covered up completely.

By mid-afternoon, he came to a tight flat valley that widened out between sheer cliffs. There was no grass in it, but there was a stream that raced its course against one wall. He made a circle of this flat, and found the remains of a campfire. Here then, was where the drive reached the first day. Riders could hold a hungry herd here through the night, each watch warming itself at a fire whose fuel had been carried for a half a day on horseback.

He went on into more canyon country, and when night came down, he picked a sheltered *rincon* off the trail and camped there. He had no food for his pony, and none for himself, and no bedroll, except the slicker. He watered his gray, rubbed him down, then rolled up in his slicker under a shelf of rock to wait the night through. He could travel well enough in the dark, but he did not want to risk losing the trail.

He was surprised the next morning that he had slept, but he remembered he had had no real rest since the bruising, exhausting fight with Petrie. He was stiff and sore and cold and hungry, and at daylight he was on the trail again, a raw wind that smelled of rain and the gray day beating in his face.

It seemed to him as he traveled between these rugged cold peaks that this country was endless, that he had never seen anything but mountains shrouded today in thunderheads. But by mid-afternoon, he could tell that he was traveling a decided downslope, and had been for hours. Soon he saw thin timber, and then timber and brush, and was finally free of the cold mountain walls. At first he could see only a great gap in the cloud-shrouded mountains, but when he was free enough for a view, he saw that this below him was a dark wide valley in a fold of these peaks. It was green below, but it was the cold green of pines and junipers ready to receive rain. The dim trail of the herd took him down the mountainside until it picked up other trails and was lost to him.

But he had seen enough. On the valley floor, he picked up a rocky, worn and wet road, and was soon making way for the huge ore wagons with their six and eight and ten horse teams that traveled it. His direction was up the valley, although he did not know why. There were a dozen rutted side-tracks that turned into the road which flanked a wide and rapid stream now. When he looked up at the forbidding mountains on either side, he could see the tiny pinpoints of nine shacks clinging to their steep sides and veiled in mist.

Not one of the crew on these huge ore wagons paid the slightest attention to him, and he took this to mean that cowmen were no strangers to this community.

Where the valley narrowed down, he found the town. It was a settlement of board shacks and tents fronting one street that was deep in mucky mud, and it was, above all, busy. The same heavy ore wagons were churning up the street, their drivers demanding way in fluent curses over the buckboards and other rigs of every description. The mist above was dissolving into a thin rain, but the men and the few women thronging the greasy board sidewalks paid no attention to it.

Flood worked his way down the jammed street to the

feed stable where he gave his tired gray over to a boy for graining. On the walk now and in the crowd composed of prospectors, townspeople, a few cattlemen, promoters, and a motley crowd of hangers-on and rusty looking miners and mule skinners, Flood paused under a wooden awning of a store. It was a pleasant din around him, colorful and tawdry and full of life. Cienega the town was named, so the sign on the criblike assay office informed him from across the street.

Now that he was here, he was at a loss as to what to do. He could not ask the names of men who had beef contracts for these camps and the town, posing as a seller himself and questioning them. If they should want beef, he would be hard put to supply them, and his mission would be detected before he had been here a day. And then he thought of his name, and the difference it had made across the mountains in Clearcreek. If stolen trail herds—perhaps the Munro herd—had ended up here, and he thought it had, then the chances were that the name Flood was not unknown. He would let that name be known then.

The Bonanza was the biggest saloon, Flood found. It had the loud steady hum of accustomed prosperity, and the free and open camaraderie of a frontier club, which it was. The bar lay to the right along the wall, and was an ornate, heavy affair of thick mahogany. The rest of the big room was shabby alongside it and its magnificent mirror.

Flood noted with mild amusement that the glasses had been so stacked on the back bar as to hide three ragged holes toward the bottom of the mirror, holes made by bullets.

All the gambling tables—poker, monte, faro—were doing a brisk business. He made his way to the bar and ordered a whisky from a rotund, jolly faced bartender.

When it was brought to him, he asked the barkeep, "A man didn't leave word for me here, did he? Flood is the name."

"Your name?"

"Yes. Any word for Flood."

The bartender, as Flood hoped he would, consulted the other three bartenders, who looked toward Flood and shook their heads negatively. Unsatisfied, the bartender called for a swamper, whom he asked to circulate with the same question among the percentage girls not busy at the time.

"In a minute, mister," the bartender said obligingly.

Flood waited, the whisky warming him and the smell of tobacco smoke and alcohol and wet wool pleasant in his nose. Around the end of the bar, the room made an elbow, and it was in this big set-back where most of the percentage girls were seated at tables with their men. There was some fitful, halfhearted music from a piano in its back corner, but it was drowned or forgotten in the talk.

His elbow on the bar, half turned, Flood was watching, when a voice said behind him, "You are Flood?"

Flood turned to find one of the percentage girls facing him. She was dark of skin with a lovely face hard as agate, and curious, surface lighted black eyes. Her dress was black, cheap, clinging, full of her curved body as she leaned against the bar.

"Yes," Flood said.

"Buy me a drink and let's take a table."

Flood gave his order and followed her into the other room. They took a table in the corner, both sitting on a rough corner bench.

"Won't you miss your man?" the girl asked.

"I don't think he's here," Flood said. When the drinks came, they both left them untouched.

"So they wouldn't bother us," the girl said, indicating the drinks.

She was studying Flood with frank, observing eyes, and finally she said quietly, "You do look like him."

"Gordie?"

"Yes. He must be your brother."

"Was," Flood corrected. "He is dead now."

The girl nodded, no expression in her face. "I know. Did he ever mention Teresa?" And when Flood made to answer, she said, "Or Tionetta? That is my real name.

I am Italian, but they want me to be Spanish, so I am. Did he?"

"I hadn't seen him for two years," Flood said. "Maybe he did, but I did not know you and missed the name."

"No. He did not know me that long before he died." She leaned back against the wall, her face gone slack and weary and somehow desperate. "You are not drinking," she said.

"No. May I get you another?"

"You have his same manners," Teresa said quietly, with an undertone of bitterness. She asked without much interest, "Have you been looking for the town all this time?"

"Off and on, yes."

"How did you find it?"

"He traveled a lot. I met someone who said he saw him here."

"Oh," she said, and again there was that look of disappointment. "And now that you have?"

"I don't know," Flood said carelessly. "I would like to find out more about it."

"Ah, then your asking if a man left word for you was just a way of getting your name around. Is that it?"

"Yes," Flood said, with a quiet smile. "Men aren't so anxious to claim his acquaintance after what happened."

"I don't think you would want to claim theirs if you knew them either."

Flood stilled his hand which was toying with the whisky glass. This was all he wanted, this knowledge that Gordie's friends were known by her.

"They got away with the cattle, didn't they?" he asked carelessly.

She looked sharply at him. "But they left him—deserted him."

"Things happen like that. I've known them to myself."

She leaned back against the wall, her eyes at once secretive and calculating. "Then you aren't hunting them?"

Flood's stare was frank, almost brutal. "That's water under the bridge. I'm hunting them, maybe, but not for what you think."

"Not to square it for Gordie?"

"No."

There was a long pause, and Teresa said, "For what then?"

Flood revolved the glass of whisky between his fingers, and did not look at her. "I've got something to sell," he said.

She started to rise, but Flood took hold of her arm and drew her down again. "Hear it out, first. I haven't seen Gordie for longer than an hour since we were kids. I don't know what he was. Maybe he deserved to get shot in the back. How do I know?"

"But he loved you!" the girl said passionately.

Flood turned away, so that she could not see the muscles in his throat tighten. Then he laughed, a little scornfully, harshly, and looked at her, his eyes jeering.

"You're breaking my heart," he mocked. He leaned toward her, his face still smiling sardonically. "Do you think I came clear here to fight a saloon floozy's battles for her?"

Before he finished, she had half risen and slapped him viciously across the mouth. Men at tables around them turned at the sound as Teresa walked away from the table. Flood glared at them and concentrated on his drink, like a surly, crestfallen puncher nursing an insult over a drink.

But inwardly, he was certain he had been right in his swift change of front to the girl. She had loved Gordie Flood, and her bitterness showed on her face. He had given his name at the bar, so many men knew his name was Flood. If talk got around that Gordon Flood's brother and sweetheart were seen talking amicably together it might reach the ears of the men he was after. It would end with a bullet in his back. As it was, he had talked with the girl just long enough to learn that she knew the names of these men, and then he had provoked her into striking him, so that the whole room might see. If word got around that Gordon Flood's brother and sweetheart had quarreled, then it would not seem that he had come here to revenge the death of his brother.

When the interest in him had died, Flood rose and left the room, walking past the bar and outside. He knew that he must talk to Teresa again, and learn what she knew of these men. Tonight, under cover of darkness and hidden from prying eyes, he would get the rest of her story—and the names he wanted.

Outside, he turned into the nearest café. He had been so eager to make sure this was the town he wanted that he had forgotten he was hungry. The café was a small one, a long counter running its length. He took a chair at the counter and ordered steak, potatoes, eggs, pie and coffee and then sat back, debating how he could best spend the little time until dark when he could see Teresa again.

He looked up when two men entered. At first sight, they looked to be cattlemen, the older and shorter one a middle-aged man in black trousers, half boots and Stetson and pearl-handled six-guns. He had a ruddy, jovial face that crinkled benevolently when he talked or stared or laughed. The other man was younger, swarthy, quieter seeming, and he wore a slicker shiny with rain.

All this Flood noticed in a glance, thinking that these two were probably a prosperous rancher in town with one of his hands. The Chinese owner of the café opened the door from the kitchen, saw the newcomers, grinned absurdly at them and went back to his work.

Flood paid no more attention to them, until he was suddenly aware that a man was sitting on either side of him. He did not have to look to know that it was the jovial man and his friend. And he did not have to guess what it meant. They wanted him.

CHAPTER FOURTEEN

FOR A MOMENT HE DEBATED whether or not to acknowledge openly that he knew why they were there, and then he decided against it. It was daylight, the streets were crowded, and they would hardly dare to take him openly.

The Chinaman brought Flood's meal, and he set about eating it with outward calm. He was not so preoccupied, however, that he missed the nod the older man gave the Chinaman, which was a signal for him to retire again to the kitchen.

Flood had a mouthful of food half way to his mouth when he paused, looked up at the Chinaman and said quietly, "You stay here, Sam."

The older man chuckled.

Flood said calmly, "These Chinese make poor witnesses, but he'll have to do. What do you want?"

"Looks like this has happened to you before," the old man said.

"Get it over."

"Not till you've eaten, Flood. I'm the town marshal. Brothers is the name. This is my deputy, Colson."

Flood said, "I'm not glad to know you." He wondered if Teresa, hating him unreasonably, had warned the marshal that he was a troublemaker looking for trouble.

Again the marshal chuckled. "I didn't reckon you would be. When you're done, we'll go over to my office."

Flood said to the Chinaman, "You stay here, I say."

He ate a leisurely meal, ignoring the silence of the two lawmen and Chinaman. When he finished, he packed his pipe and lighted it and paid for the meal, then said, "I'm ready."

The three of them walked down the street a half block and entered a lighted office. It was a large, bare room, with a stairway running up to the second floor and, Flood supposed, to the jail.

Colson was last in, and he locked the street door, although the wide uncurtained window fronting the street showed anyone wanting to look that the room was occupied.

"Sit down," Brothers invited, indicating one of the three straight backed chairs cluttered around the big desk under the light.

Flood sat down and tilted his chair against the wall, shifting his gun up on his lap.

"This is just customary," Brothers said diffidently. "Word got around that a Flood was in town expecting somebody. That right?"

"That's right."

Brothers leaned against the desk and regarded Flood with quiet curiosity. "Who?"

"A man I was going to pick mushrooms with," Flood said. "I met him in Mexico two years ago and we made a date to meet here."

The marshal didn't smile. "You ain't a lot different from Gordie, are you?"

"I wouldn't know that," Flood said, smiling a little.

The marshal glared at him. Flood yawned. Colson cleared his throat and leaned against the door.

"I've heard of men jokin' themselves into bad jams," Brothers said calmly.

"And I've seen curiosity get men into worse ones," Flood retorted with mildness.

"The law has to have a certain amount of that."

"A certain amount, yes," Flood conceded.

The marshal was silent a moment, as if puzzling how to say what he was going to. Then he said, "We never thought much of your brother here."

Flood nodded politely.

"You know how he was killed, don't you?" the marshal continued.

"Rustling," Flood said calmly.

"Yes." The marshal paused, choosing his words. "He had it coming to him. He was a rat. If I thought you were in this town hunting the men responsible for his death, I wouldn't like it very much."

Flood looked up at him with a wide, surprised stare. "That's queer," he said slowly. "I heard that Gordie was killed by the Munro riders. Hanged."

"He was," Brothers said evenly. "But the story got around some way that these men he was riding with left him stranded on the back trail—took his horse, so he'd have to fight and couldn't run."

Flood raised his eyebrows politely. "And these men are here, you say?"

"I didn't say it," Brothers said patiently. "I said I wouldn't like it much if you started hunting them to square things. There's nothing to square."

Flood said, "I think I see."

"I thought you would," Brothers said gently.

To Flood, this was broad enough warning to mind his own business, and a warning, too, that these men who had run with Gordie were in this town, and that Brothers and Colson knew them and were protecting them. Which meant, of course, that Brothers and Colson were very probably two of the gang who had taken the Munro herd and the Shifflin herd. Flood did not betray that any of this was of much interest to him.

He said carelessly, "I think you've got me wrong."

"How?" Brothers said.

"Well," Flood said slowly, studying his boot toe, "I remember having a brother by the name of Gordon. I haven't seen him twice since we were grown up. I don't give a damn if he was hanged, shot, knifed, or poisoned, or if he's alive or dead. I've traveled a good bit of country in my time, and in some towns I've had to change my name because my brother had been there before me and they were ready to lynch anyone by the name of Flood."

He looked up at the sheriff. "I suppose you are trying to tell me he had enemies. I don't doubt that. But if I know Gordie, the men he ran with are much more likely to be looking for me than I am to be looking for them. He had a way of making people hate him and the name he bore. As a matter of fact, I'd be obliged if you didn't spread it around that my name is Flood. It might be safer for me."

Plainly, the marshal was puzzled. He looked over at Colson and then back at Flood, and his ruddy, amiable face was wary.

"What are you here for then?" Brothers asked bluntly.

Flood said blandly, "I just drifted up ahead of a Texas trail herd. I'm supposed to join them over east when they pass. Anything wrong with that?" He watched their faces to see if they showed any interest, but he saw nothing except caution.

"This is way off any trail—way, way off," Brothers said.

"Isn't it, though?" Flood said pleasantly, and he let it go at that.

Presently, Brothers said, "That's interesting. But it don't change the advice I was going to give you."

"Yes?"

"You ought to take it," Brothers said. "A man never suffered from listening to this kind of advice."

"I'm listening," Flood said.

"I wouldn't stay here any longer than I could help," Brothers said slowly.

Flood nodded. "I've listened to that kind before. Thanks anyway."

"Sure," Brothers said softly, amiably.

Flood stood up. "Is that all?"

"I reckon," the marshal said.

Colson unlocked the door and stood to one side. Flood bid them both good day and sauntered out into the street, and turned toward the Bonanza. It was almost dark now, and several of the stores were lighted for the night.

He considered the marshal and his warning. He did not know if Brothers believed him when he disclaimed Gordie, but he thought he did. Flood was certain that Brothers was one of the trail rustlers, and he hoped Brothers would repeat their conversation to his friends. He hoped this for two reasons: he did not want these men to think he was here to revenge Gordie, and he wanted Brothers to tell them of the trail herd which was coming. If he could leave the impression with Brothers that he was on the lookout for men such as Gordie ran with to help him with the same kind of job that Gordie was killed in doing, then and then alone would he best be able to get into their confidence. And in the meantime, he must see Teresa and find out if she knew these men, and if she would give him their names. Brothers's warning to leave town was merely the act of a cautious man. Flood did not take it seriously.

When he entered the Bonanza again, the evening crowd of miners was there, and the place was doing a booming and noisy business. He wondered how he might best get in touch with Teresa, knowing that he didn't dare speak to her, and disliking to write her a note and trust it to a messenger he did not know. A note would implicate him as no speech with Teresa ever would.

Drifting over to one of the gambling tables, he saw her at a table far across the room in company with two men. She was watching the room too, and he wondered if she were looking for him. On the chance that she might be, he strolled over to the bar. Most of the customers had left the bar for the gambling tables, so he picked a clear place toward the end of the bar and ordered a whisky.

In a moment, he saw her leave her table with a man and come toward the bar. Flood studied his drink.

When she came to the bar next him, he looked up, and she saw him at the same time.

He smiled. "Hallo."

She stared at him stonily, then turned to the man on the other side of her. Flood inwardly cursed his foolishness. He should have had a note written which he could have placed in her hand as he left. She was joking now with her man, laughing hoarsely at something the fellow was telling her in a low tone.

Flood holding his whisky glass loosely in his left hand, suddenly felt his arm bumped. The whisky sloshed over the glass from the impact. He turned to find a wiry little man next him. The man was smiling amiably, apologetically.

"I'm sorry about that, mister." He said to the bartender, "George, another whisky for this gent."

Before Flood could protest or say anything, there was a fresh drink poured in his glass and paid for. The little man, wizened, erect, with a face as brown and tight over his cheekbones as new leather, raised his glass.

"Here's to steady legs. I could never manage 'em."

Flood drank with him, smiling.

"You're new here too, ain't you?" the little man asked, and there was no offensiveness in the question. Flood told him he was.

"Then you wouldn't be any help," the little man said, with as much glumness as his high spirits could manage.

"Not much," Flood conceded. "What for, though?"

"Well, you looked like a cowman," the man said, looking over Flood's dress. "So am I. I got some money, and I ain't awfully drunk, and I want a poker game. But these miners ain't poker men. They got one table over there, but the limit is clean over my head. I thought maybe another cowman could show me a small limit poker game, but I reckon there ain't any."

The bartender, with business temporarily slack, was leaning against the back bar, his arms folded. He was the same one that Flood had questioned earlier. He smiled at the small man. "There's a couple of back rooms," he said, with a nod of his head toward the rear of the saloon. "Get a few of your friends and see Claborne. He'll likely dig up a house man for you."

"Who's Claborne?" the small man asked.

The bartender looked over the room, then said, "That big gent with the black coat and gray hair standin' by the table. He owns the place."

The small man nodded and started across the room to the owner. Flood saw them speak to each other, and Claborne nodded. Then Flood saw him go over to a group standing around the poker table watching. He talked to three men who nodded and they all started for a back room. Suddenly, the little man paused, as if remembering something, and came back to the bar. Flood knew he was coming for him. He noticed then that Teresa was gone, and the bartender was about his business again.

And right there, Flood decided this had been planned, rehearsed. Teresa had come to the bar to point him out to the small man, who had put over his act with convincing finesse. The bartender had been handy to make the suggestion, Claborne to give consent, the other three men to assent to the game. It was a round-about, skillful way to get him in a back room.

Before the small man reached him, Flood had framed his answer.

The small man said, "I just happened to remember you might like to sit in. This gent Claborne fixed it up for a back room."

"I've only got twelve dollars," Flood said pleasantly.

"Hell, I've only got fifteen, if that's all that's stoppin' you."

"I'd like to," Flood said.

Flood followed him through the crowded room to the entrance of a small corridor that knifed the back wall under the stairs leading to the second floor. The small man stopped.

"Where'd they go?"

"I didn't notice," Flood said.

The small man went on down the corridor. At the first door he came to he paused and opened it. Five men around a poker table looked up, and the small man muttered apologies, backing out. At the second door down the corridor he did the same, then swung it open and stood aside for Flood.

Flood entered the room. Five men stood against the back wall, silently observing him. Teresa stood in the middle. A green-felted, round table stood under the circle of strong light from an overhead oil lamp. Flood heard the door close behind him.

"I wondered when you would get the word," he said calmly, smiling a little at Teresa.

"Is that him?" one man said.

"Yes," Teresa answered.

Flood already had seen a door in the back wall of the room, and he supposed it let out into the night. Teresa had come in that way, for small silver drops of rain beaded her hair. Without looking, he knew the small man behind him had a gun out and was leaning against the door. And without thinking, too, he knew he had waited too long to tell Teresa the truth.

CHAPTER FIFTEEN

MARGOT RODE BLINDLY AWAY from Hartley's cabin. She had learned suddenly the meaning of serenity, and she thought of all those little things by which she had arrived at loving him—his justice, which was as implacable in generosity as it was in punishment, and she thought this was what had first made her think him a man apart, and to be loved. She thought of his eyes, so like hers, and yet which could no more bear dishonor and deceit than a visible conscience. They had angered her that first day when he came to her at the hotel, angered her because they were so unlike everything she knew about the name he bore.

But now she understood him, without knowing why he was here or what it was he had to do, and she told herself she understood it with just the few gentle, meager words he had used when he held her in his arms. She tried to doubt, to disbelieve him, so that she could test herself, but her understanding was too great. Without his ever saying it, she knew there was something that made up his pride and his conscience and his honor, forcing him to do this before he could come to her the way he wanted. And she could wait.

And then she laughed at herself because she was making a knight out of her man, who, after all, would make human mistakes like herself.

It was only when she heard horses approaching that

she quieted herself. Then she pulled her horse off into the thicket along the road and dismounted quietly and put her hand over her horse's nose so that he would not whicker.

She caught the deliberate rhythm of the passing horses, two of them. Mayhew and Honeywell on their fruitless errand. Listening to the sound die, she thought proudly of how Mark had won the loyalty of these two men, as he won everybody's.

But, back on the road again, she sobered. There was still that shadow before her of the man she had almost married, the man she once thought she loved: Petrie. She marveled at how wrong she had been, how dangerously wrong.

She was afraid of him, and the dark, violent side of him he had hidden so well. Flood had seen it instantly, and was unwilling to leave until he knew she was safe.

And that reminded her: Should she wait for Honeywell? No. Anyone seeing the three of them ride into town together would think it odd, and repeat his thoughts. This was one thing that must never get to Petrie, for it was a move that might defeat him in the end. She would tell him this sometime, when she told him she loved Flood, and that she had done this to save the man she loved. With Flood, she would not be afraid. Alone, she was.

But, afraid or not, she knew she could not wait for Honeywell, but must ride in alone. What if Petrie was still in town? What if he had tried to reach her after Honeywell and Mayhew left to serve the warrants? She didn't know, but she would have to take that chance.

She did not enter the dark town from this road, but traveled the ridge a mile, then dropped down into the valley and rode in from this direction.

The town was quiet and dark, except for a few lights burning in the rear of stores. As she passed the hotel she saw the lamp turned low on the lobby desk. She turned in at the feed stable and gave her horse over to the night boy, who went on duty at midnight.

"Any trouble tonight, Jim?"

"No, Miss Curtin. Only them Wagon Hammer men in here an hour or so ago. They didn't make trouble."

She could only see the shape of him here in the dark, and knew that he could not see her. So she asked, "What happened tonight, Jim? Does anybody know?"

His answer was long in coming, "Yes, ma'am."

"What is it?" And when he did not answer immediately, she said, "I'm sorry. Maybe that's none of my business."

"It ain't that," the boy said quietly out of the night. "Coe, a Bar Stirrup rider, along with a bunch of other men, stampeded most of the Wagon Hammer herds over the Barrier Rim. But that ain't the worst part, Miss Curtin."

"Not the worst?"

"No. They had to kill the seven men ridin' herd on the Wagon Hammer stuff before they could do it."

Margot felt a weary horror rise up within her.

"Oh, it was a terrible, terrible mistake." She thought of the warrant out for Hand, and knew this was the cause.

"I reckon Hand will find that out, ma'am," the boy said, his voice sounding choked. "My dad was one of 'em. None of them seven were Wagon Hammer men, but that didn't make no difference. They were killed—shot in the back, without a chance to fight."

Margot came close to him and laid a hand on his arm. "I'm terribly sorry for you, Jim, and your mother. But perhaps Ben Hand didn't order it done. We don't know yet. He was in jail, you know."

"He could've give orders before he went to jail," the boy said, and his voice was adamant.

Margot pressed his hand. "Jim, every man in this country will go killing crazy. Are you going to, too?"

"I reckon," the boy said stubbornly, respectfully.

"Then I'm doubly sorry for you," Margot said gently. "Good night, Jim."

"Good night, Miss Curtin."

As she crossed the dark street, Margot began to piece together the things she had overheard that night. When

she rode up to Hartley's cabin she had heard Ben
Hand's voice calling out in anger. Mark had known of
this terrible thing, and had refused to tell her what it
was. Had he been quarreling with Hand over it? A fear
rose in her, but she stilled it. Something was wrong, all
wrong. Hadn't Honeywell given her leave to warn Ben
Hand, too? And did not that prove that neither Mayhew nor Honeywell believed them guilty? But when she
thought of the fire this would touch off among the families on this range, she was sick. And to head this in-
jured faction would be Petrie, who would use their
anger and their blood to win his quarrel with Ben
Hand.

All Margot's light-heartedness of an hour ago had
turned into a wild longing for Flood. But she knew that
she would have to conquer this, because her only free-
dom lay in patience, a patience that would bring him
to her eventually. She entered the hotel and heard how
weary her footsteps sounded in echo. Her fear of being
alone was gone now, supplanted by the news Jim had
told her.

Passing the desk, she moved the lamp against the wall
and turned it very low, then walked back to her room.
Here, she moved in the dark with the confidence of
familiarity. Lighting her lamp, she wondered if Lee
was awake in the next room. He had been asleep when
Honeywell came to see her, and she had not wakened
him; but now she wondered if he might not want to
hear all this. She decided against waking him, remembering how his frail body needed sleep and rest.

She turned away from the lamp on the stand near her
bed, drawing off her left glove. Then she stopped
abruptly as she caught sight of her dresser. Its drawers
were open, the contents piled awry on the top. A trunk
under the window serving as a seat had been opened,
and papers were scattered about.

Seeing it, she felt her spine go cold with fear. She ran
to the trunk, dropped on her knees and started pawing
frantically in a back corner of it. Then she stopped, and
slowly picked up a slim sheaf of letters that lay on top

the heap of clothes.

Rising, her face white and taut, she ran across the room out into the corridor, and broke into her brother's room. "Lee! Lee! They know! They've found out!"

It was dark, here, and quiet. She paused, waiting for him to rouse from sleep and answer her. When he did not, she moved swiftly across the room to his bed and shook him, saying, "Lee! Lee!"

He did not move. A crawling, growing terror started within her. She fumbled at the table, found a match, dropped it in her haste, and found another and struck it, turning to the bed while the match still flared.

Then her scream rose and filled all silence with its terror. The match still burned. Lee might have been looking at it, for his head was turned that way, his eyes open. In the middle of his forehead was a jagged bullet hole.

The next Margot knew, the cook was standing in the door, shapeless in a vast sleazy wrap. She had a lamp in her hand, and her face was still loose with sleep. Margot ran to her.

Jim, the stable boy, was next in, and Mrs. Cooney motioned him to the bed.

"Tell Sam Honeywell," she said. She led Margot down the corridor into her own small, plain room, and moved her over to the bed. Margot lay on it, face down, crying brokenly, while Mrs. Cooney put the lamp on the table. She watched Margot, her plain, motherly face alive with sympathy. Then she sat on the bed, her back against the foot of it, and gathered Margot into her arms.

Sam Honeywell and Max Mayhew found them that way, after Jim had hunted vainly for them at the office and both their houses, and had come back to find them riding into town.

Mrs. Cooney motioned them away, then got up and closed the door. Mayhew looked at Sam in the dark corridor.

"That ain't part of this fight," he said quietly.

"No," Sam said. "I think this is my fault, Max."

"No. Flood would never have expected this, nor will he blame you."

He went back to Lee's room, while Honeywell leaned against the corridor wall and waited. When the door opened, Margot stepped out. Sam took his hat off and began to speak, and Margot said, "I know, Sam. Go in the room and wait for me."

She went on up the corridor, Honeywell watching her, and turned into her own room. In a moment she returned to Mrs. Cooney's room, and Mrs. Cooney left. Honeywell stood by the bed, his face more sad than usual.

Margot sat lifelessly in a chair, and Sam said, "You want to talk, Miss Margot?"

She nodded, feeling the slim sheaf of letters inside her blouse, fighting the grief out of her mind so that she could answer his questions. "You know all I do, Sam. I found him just that way."

Sam could be blunt when he wanted to—and he wanted to now. "Petrie could have had a man watching you when you left town. Maybe he knew. Maybe that's his revenge." He studied her clean, modeled head as she listened to this, and when she looked up at him he was proud of her.

"Sam, you know all that's passed. Do you think Loosh would do that?"

"Do you?"

"No. I guessed wrong about him once, Sam, but not that far wrong."

Sam said nothing, waiting for her to go on.

"It was robbery," Margot said simply. "My dresser and trunk were rifled."

"I saw that, coming in," Sam said, and he saw the swift shadow of surprise and fear cross her face. Something in him rebelled at this, and he knew he could never help her, but he went on placidly, "That don't explain Lee. Why would they rob your stuff and kill Lee while he slept?"

Margot said, "I don't know."

Sam's voice got a little stronger, but it was still gentle.

"Something they found made it necessary to get Lee out of the way. Wasn't that it?"

Margot said, without looking at him, "It's reasonable, I—"

"Don't lie," Sam said kindly. "You know what it was. You went back to get it." He sighed and sat down on the bed, hat in hand between his knees. He spoke conversationally now, and there was no hint of reproof in what he said, "You and Lee come here a year ago, Margot. Nobody knew where from, although you both said the East. You bought this hotel and lived here in this little cow town as if you meant to make yourself like it the rest of your life. I've often asked myself why."

She was watching him now with cautious, kind eyes, saying nothing.

He went on. "You didn't come here because you liked it, or because you heard of it. You came here for something. I've thought that a long time, and never said it." He juggled his hat a little and looked up at her, his heavy, strong face alert now. "You won't say why you come. You won't say where you come from. All right. I reckon that means you don't want our help much, don't it?"

Margot said, "Sam, I—"

He cut her off by raising a hand. "Don't tell me anything you don't want me to remember." His hand dropped gently, and he smiled. "I can be a curious man; and, then, again, I can't. I never aimed to be a righteous lawman. I'm one that thinks a lot of killings are meant to ride that way, that everyone is better off if they go unsolved. It's a logical way to settle a lot of things, and if some men are driven to doing it, then their way should be respected. Some men, understand? Most killings, though, are bad. I knew Lee, and I wouldn't say he had ever done anything that called for this. Has he?"

"No," Margot said, her voice faint.

"And still you don't want our help?"

Margot stood up suddenly, clasped her hands in front of her and walked across the room. She paused before a blank wall, turned and walked back to Sam. Leaning against the foot of the bed, she said, "Yes, Sam, I want your help; but not in this."

"All right."

"I have got to get out of here," she said slowly, trying to make her voice calm. "I can't tell you why, Sam, but as soon as Lee is buried, I have got to go."

Sam said quietly, meaning no question, "To Flood."

"Yes."

He looked up at her. "You're afraid."

"Yes."

"Even with me around, like I promised you and Flood I would be?"

"It's past that now, Sam," she answered, a note of hysteria creeping into her voice in spite of all she could do.

"What is it?" Sam said sharply.

Margot covered her face with her hands. "Oh, Sam, I can't tell you. It wouldn't do any good, and it would only pull you into it, too. I don't care now. All I want is to be free." She looked pleadingly at him, and for a moment pity seemed to gag him to silence.

"Sam, I don't want to die. Before tonight, I wouldn't have cared; but now I don't want to. I can't." She quieted herself and said more calmly, "Do you believe, Sam, that you have to snatch and steal and fight for all the happiness you can get in this world?"

"Some people do."

"I'm one of them, Sam. Oh, I know it sounds cheap for me to say this, with Lee in there. But he's past help. He died because—on account of this thing that I'm running away from. But I don't care now. I love Mark! With him I can come back and fight it. But, without him, I'll die."

"Be killed, you mean," Sam said.

"Yes."

Sam said kindly, "Sure this ain't made you imagine things?"

"No," she said earnestly. "Please believe me. No. Lee's body in there will tell you how little I imagine it."

Sam nodded, looking at his hat, studying the fat,

strong fingers that held it. He said, without looking at Margot, "I reckon you know that you are riding to join a wanted man. If he ever comes back to this range, we'll have to pick him up."

"Do you believe that charge, Sam?"

"No. That ain't the point. Petrie brought in a little rat-faced man from God-knows-where tonight who claims he was a rider with the Munro herd when Gordie Flood's gang rustled it. This man says Mark Flood was riding for Munro, too, and that Mark was the man who suggested Munro use this Ruidoso trail into the American. He says Flood had his brother's gang waiting there to steal the herd."

"Do you believe it?" Margot asked in a small voice.

"No. But it's evidence enough to pick Flood up for questioning. Only trouble is, if he ever got inside this town again Petrie would ride in here and get him. I'm telling you this because that's the man you aim to join— a man who has to travel at night or clear out of the country. Do you still want to?"

"Of course."

Sam juggled his hat now, watching her. It took plenty of courage to tell her this next, and he wanted to draw strength from her, from the clean, proud looks of her. He said then, "I saw Emory out at Hartley's."

Margot said nothing.

Sam said, "You ought to know this. God knows I don't like to tell you."

"What?"

"Hand and Emory claim that Flood set Coe up to this stampede and massacre. Hand is through with him, Emory says."

"That's not so," Margot said. She was feeling no fear, and she watched herself for a beginning of doubt, but it never came.

"I'm just telling you," Sam said.

"Do you or Mayhew believe that?" Margot asked.

"Hartley and Flood denied it."

Margot touched Sam's shoulder. "Sam, are you beginning to regret letting Mark go? Do you think you made a mistake?"

Sam said, "Not if you don't."

"Then believe in him, Sam. He's all I've got. I think he's all you've got, too, if you only knew it. If any man can avenge poor Lee, or if any man can help me, he is the man."

CHAPTER SIXTEEN

SAM AND MAYHEW had plenty of time to talk it over in the blacksmith shop, waiting for Dave Wolff to make the coffin. They sat on a bench near the forge while Dave worked in the back end by the light of a kerosene lamp with tools that were strange to his rough hands. Mayhew had listened to Sam's account of Margot's action with a shrewd, silent gravity, nodding occasionally. When Sam was finished, they fell silent, talking only now and then.

Mayhew said on one of those occasions, "There's one thing that makes me believe she is really afraid." He pointed over his shoulder to the casket. "She loved that boy and, now he's gone, she's leaving—fast."

Sam nodded, and did not speak. He rolled a cigarette in fingers that hid the paper, even hid the movements; but when he put it in his mouth it was round and firm and delicate. Day was graying the street outside, and already the fresh wet smell of morning was sifting through the wide shop door.

"In the end," Sam said, "we couldn't protect her. She knows that."

"No. Maybe it's best," Mayhew said. "If she can get to Flood, that is."

Sam said, "Do men kill women?" quizzically, curiously. "I mean, men we know. Would they ever kill women?"

"I'm older than you, Sam—old enough to admit I'm not sure about a lot of things I was."

"They killed him, and they'll kill her, she thinks. Reckon she's right?"

"She ought to know. She don't spook easy, and she don't lie."

Sam grunted, perhaps meaning nothing, and sat motionless, musing. Soon he called back to the blacksmith, "How long, Dave?"

"Fifteen-twenty minutes."

Sam said, "I'll go along."

At the feed stable he found the team hitched to the buckboard. He asked if the boys were in yet, and Jim said, yes, that they had finished.

"The ground's soft out there. No rocks," Jim explained, and added somberly, "I'll find out today."

Sam looked at his youthful face and the square set of the bony jaw and the hard eyes, sober, serious and cold.

"Rather I'd tell your ma about it, Jim? She don't know, does she?"

The boy looked at him in bitter fury. "I'll tell her myself! You get hold of Hand again. I'll see he don't walk out again like he did last night."

Sam's slack, sad face did not change, and he said nothing, so that the boy turned away, a little ashamed of his outburst.

"Drive the team down to Dave's and then go home," Sam told him.

He crossed to the hotel in the half light and found Margot in her room. She was dressed in a buckskin skirt and thick wool blouse and jacket. She was sitting quietly on her bed when Sam knocked, and she bade him come in.

He saw her eyes were dry and steady, but they held a sadness that Sam hated.

"If you could wait a while, we'd have a preacher here for him."

"No one knew him well, Sam, except you, perhaps. I—I don't want strange people mourning him."

"Steady," Sam said.

"I'm all right," she said tonelessly.

"The rig will be around in back pretty soon. You better tell Mrs. Cooney to fix you something to eat."

"All right."

Sam felt a quiet rage throttling him when he looked at her and saw how this had broken her. But he knew that in the end she was unconquerable, and that comforted him somewhat.

"What do you aim to do with this place while you're away?" he asked.

"Mrs. Cooney will run it. She can. I don't care."

She went out. He went down to his office, leading his horse down the street from in front of the hotel and tying it. It was light enough to see in the office now without a lamp, and he plodded to the gun rack. He paused in front of it and considered the array of shotguns and carbines and rifles. He chose a Winchester with a long octagon barrel and levered it open. There were two shells in it. Hefting it, he sighted it, then walked out and rammed it in his saddle scabbard. The boot was made for a shorter gun, so that it stuck up and out farther than it should have. He considered this a moment in silence, his slack face musing, then he dismissed it.

When he saw the buckboard back up to the blacksmith shop to receive its load, he turned up to the hotel again.

He found Mrs. Cooney and told her to go in with Margot. Mayhew came presently, and they went through the long corridor to the back door and waited for Dave to drive down the alley and pull up.

They carried the coffin in, Dave shambling along with a hammer in his belt and some heavy nails jingling in his dirty shoeing apron. The job was quickly done, and Sam winced for Margot when Dave drove his nails into the staunch coffin, the measured sound of his hammer racketing through the lower floor of the building.

"This ain't the first one of these I'll make today, nor tomorrow," Dave said into his grimy, sandy mustache. Then, upon further consideration, he added, "Nor for a hell of a while yet."

They maneuvred the coffin out into the buckboard, where Dave said, "I'll drive out for you if you ain't got a man."

Sam said all right, and Dave untied his apron and put on a dark coat over his hunched and broad shoulders. It had been under the buckboard seat. He had done this so many times, Sam thought, that his kindness had got to be a habit. An old man, who knew how to keep silent. Sam was glad of that.

"Drive around in front, Dave. We'll be with you in a minute."

They got Margot and Mrs. Cooney and went out. Margot was on horseback, as were Sam and Mayhew. Mrs. Cooney rode with Dave. It was full light when they left the main street and took the road south that wound out of the valley to where the hills widened out a mile from town. It was a flat stretch of ground, shaded by evergreens, a small shelf scooped out of the hillside. The morning sun was just touching the ridge of the hill behind it. Through the trees could be seen the pine headstones of a few graves. There was a mound of new earth farther back in the grove, and Dave drove to this and pulled up a little way from it.

He took off his hat, as did Sam and Mayhew. Dave took the ropes from the bottom of the wagon, snubbed them to the tree closest the grave, then stretched them taut across the top of the grave and held them.

Honeywell and Mayhew placed the coffin across the ropes, while Dave leaned back, pulling to keep the ropes tight.

Sam turned to Margot, his eyes questioning.

"Go ahead, Sam," she said. He unsnubbed the rope from the tree, and with Dave at the other end of the rope, he let the coffin slowly down into the grave.

Margot came up, looked down at it, her mouth quivering. The others watched her in silence as she picked up a handful of dirt.

"God bless you," she said simply, and dropped the dirt into the pit in a wholly sad, wholly complete gesture that made Sam turn his head away.

She walked back to her horse, and Dave came up to her along with Sam and, later, the sheriff.

"I'll 'tend to the marker, Miss Curtin," he said.

"Thank you, Dave." She looked at the others, too. "You are all kind to me."

Dave instructed Mrs. Cooney to take the team back, and he walked over to get the shovel from the buckboard.

Sam said to Margot, "You're riding away now?"

"Yes. I won't go back, Sam."

She kissed Mrs. Cooney and squeezed her hand, then mounted.

"Let Max ride with you a ways," Sam suggested.

Margot paused. "All right. Just a little ways. I'm going alone, you know."

"I know," Sam said.

She shook hands with him, and Sam saw her eyes were half wet and dark with grief, but she smiled at him before she turned her horse and rode off with Mayhew.

Sam watched them go south while Mrs. Cooney started back to town with the buckboard. The sun was half way down the hill now, Sam noticed, as he walked back toward the grave. Dave was already pushing in the dirt.

He stopped work when Sam came up.

"Dave, Max will be back in a little while. You tell him to go on in. Tell him I rode toward town."

Dave regarded him soberly, a trace of a question in his eyes, but he said he would.

"Just forget which way I rode off, will you, Dave?"

Dave nodded and watched him mount and ride toward the hill.

It was a stiff climb for his horse, but Sam let him take it easy. Once on top, he traveled along the ridge south until he came to some tracks, fresh tracks. He dismounted then and followed the tracks, which led down the hill he had just come up. Where they ended, Sam looked through the trees. He could see the graveyard below, could see Dave filling in the grave with steady, silent labor. Here, then, was where somebody had been watching.

"She was right, then," Sam said briefly, almost aloud.

He hurried back to his horse. The far slope of this ridge stretched down to an open pasture between it and another higher ridge. Sam remembered this ridge he was on flattened out to the south, and the next ridge did the same. So he headed for the next ridge, keeping in the screening timber, reached it, crossed over to its far slope and traveled perhaps two miles along its side. When it began to lose height rapidly, he dismounted and went ahead on foot, the long rifle in his fat hand.

The place where he stopped was a nest of boulders overlooking a thin thread of trail that wound around the edge of this ridge between it and a high, abrupt mesa to the south. He laid the gun down and took out his handkerchief and mopped the sweat from his face. He was breathing hard in slow, long heaves, so he sat down.

He watched the trail with flat, incurious eyes. Ten minutes passed before he caught sight of her. Her horse was trotting briskly. She made a fine picture, Sam thought, riding erect and easy, her grace lovelier to look at than her horse's. He could follow her course, missing her now and then as she passed from sight behind the scrub piñon on the hill in front of him, but then he saw her again. He watched these spots where she disappeared from sight, noting them. He noted, too, an open stretch clear of trees where she quartered toward him for several long seconds, only far below.

He remembered that, even reached down and took the long-barreled rifle and sighted at nothing in that long, open stretch. Then he let his rifle rest that way and rolled himself a cigarette which he smoked peacefully, shivering a little because the sun would not touch his side of this ridge till it was much higher.

It was longer than ten minutes before he leaned forward again. He dropped his cigarette, looked at the sky, then took off his hat and laid a hand on the rifle. A man was riding the trail below. There was something alert about his seat in the saddle, something wary and nervous. He was traveling a little slower than Margot had been, as if these hills demanded a little caution.

Sam observed him with a still, meditative gaze. He picked his cigarette up, dragged in one long, sweet, cracking drag and laid it down. Then he bellied down and made himself comfortable. He took two trial sights on the open place, squirmed a little, then stilled himself, waiting.

Presently he raised the rifle butt to his shoulder and laid his cheek along the stock. It was so fat that it bulged out over the curved upper edge of the stock and almost closed his eye. But he looked down between the twin lines that led his squint out to the end sight and over it. When the man appeared from behind the trees, Sam first put the whole sight on his shirtfront, then, remembering truly that a man overshoots downhill, he eased the nose of the rifle down until the front sight was fine in the crotch of the rear sight. And then he eased it down some more until the sight was fine, very fine, in the center of the man's belly. He was already squeezing the pistol grip hard, so that the shot came almost as a surprise. The barrel flicked up then, blotting out what he wanted to see, but he knew his aim had been perfect.

When he stood up and looked, the man was on the ground, on his back, and his horse had stopped almost beside him.

Sam picked up his cigarette and tried to suck it to life, but it was out. He lighted it and then, remembering that he had lighted one before, he found the match and put that one and the new match in his pocket. He didn't bother to lever the shell out of his gun. When he had made sure he was leaving no tracks, he turned back toward his horse.

He didn't bother to go down and look at the man. He knew he was dead. He knew, too, who the man was, and he found a kind of comfortable and stern relish in the thought that he had been wanting to do just this thing to Breckenridge for a long time.

"She deserves a chance, anyway," Sam thought as he paused to regard the sky. Yes, the day would be clear.

CHAPTER SEVENTEEN

IN THAT FIRST QUIET MOMENT of facing these men, Flood knew that Teresa had betrayed him in order to save herself. These were the trail rustlers, and Flood did not doubt that Teresa had told them he was in town to avenge Gordie's death.

He drew a long, deep breath and singled out the leader, the man who had asked Teresa the question. The other men waited for him to speak, and kept glancing at him. Like them, he was dressed in soiled waist overalls, flannel shirt, greasy Stetson and half boots, and, like them, he wore a gun at his hip. But, unlike them, he was unshaven, and his eyes were a little whisky veined. Flood noted the loose face padded with fat and unsupported by the sagging muscles. His lips were thick and parted and his eyes so greedy they drew all his other features into giving the impression of a swine's face.

This man said, "Sit down."

Flood pulled a chair out and sat down. So did this man, although Teresa and the others stood.

"I hear you're looking for your brother's friends," the man said surlily.

"Have you talked to Brothers?" Flood asked easily.

"I talked to him," the man said. "Then Teresa got hold of me. So you're looking for Gordie's friends, huh?"

"Sure I am," Flood said openly. "It took you long enough to find me."

"Be careful, Klaus," Teresa said coldly.

Flood looked up at her, his face thoughtful, then he looked at Klaus.

"She told you, didn't she?" he asked slowly.

Klaus smiled uglily. "Sure, she told us."

Flood spread his hands. "Well, then, let's talk business. I can spot you the trail herd—the date they'll pass, the number of men, everything you want to know. If you can get rid of—"

"Wait a minute," Klaus cut in. "What are you talking about?"

Flood looked again at Teresa, and this time he scowled. He said to Klaus, "Didn't she tell you?"

Klaus laughed shortly. "Yeah—that you was lookin' for the men that was in trouble with Gordie."

"I am."

No one spoke for a moment, then Klaus said, "She said you aimed to square things with us over Gordie's death. She said you aimed to gun the whole bunch of us if you could find us."

Flood looked up at Teresa, and his eyes were hard. "What's the game?"

"He's lying, Klaus!" Teresa said savagely. "He hunted me out and asked me if I knew the men Gordie ran with, and when I told him I might and asked him why he wanted to know, he just put his hand on his gun and smiled!"

It was a skillful lie, skillfully told, Flood saw, and it was told in desperation, because Teresa believed that Flood would eventually find these men and tell them of her hatred for them. She had betrayed Flood before he could betray her, and although he pitied her and admired her courage, he saw that she had started a play he must finish.

So what he said now was without pity, and was as cold and cutting and convincing as he could make it. He said, "You've cut your own throat. You hunted me up in the barroom and you made me the proposition. You thought I had come here to even scores for Gordie, and you talked without finding out the real facts. You offered to point these men out to me if I would kill them. When I refused, you slapped my face and left me. And because you were afraid I'd double-cross you, you lied to these men so they would get me out of the way before I could talk. You named Brothers and Colson as two of these men. I parleyed with them and told them why I was really here. But you thought you could talk to these men before I could move."

He leaned back now and said, "You asked for this. Talk yourself out of it."

Teresa's face had hardened, but she had perfect control over herself. Speaking to Klaus, she said, "Believe him, and you're a dead man, Klaus."

"Talk to Brothers," Flood said gently. "Find out why I'm here. When I first came in here, I thought she had told you the truth—that I wanted to talk business with you. Ask Brothers about that."

Klaus drummed on the table in slow, thoughtful monotony. Then he turned ponderously in his chair and said to Teresa, "How would he know about Brothers if you didn't tell him?"

"I did mention Brothers!" Teresa lied desperately. "I told him to go to Brothers and work with him, because Brothers was hunting the same men he was. I knew Brothers would take care of him before he could do any harm. At least I hoped he would."

Flood calmly contradicted her, "You lie. You told me Brothers and Colson were two of the men responsible for Gordie's death. When I told you I wasn't here for that, and that I wanted them to help me swing a business deal, you slapped my face." He hammered this home, knowing it was the chief proof of what he was saying. "If you doubt that," he said to Klaus, "ask a dozen men in that barroom out there. They saw her hit me."

One of the men said to Klaus, "I saw it, Klaus. Over at that corner table with the benches."

Klaus was utterly still for a moment, then he rose and faced Teresa. "I should have knowed better than to believe you. I thought you'd forget that rat of a Gordie. I guess you haven't."

Flood saw the fear in her eyes, and he knew she was cornered, and that from now on it would be a hopeless bluff for her. He wanted to warn her, to tell her to leave because these men would kill her; but he understood that she knew all this. She was playing a game for her life, and knew it.

Now she laughed easily. "All right, Klaus. You did me a good turn once when you brought Gordie to me. We weren't together very long; but I loved him, and I was glad for the little time I had. I was grateful to you, too, and tried to show it tonight. When you get a slug in your back, it will be too late for you to say you were wrong."

Klaus only signaled with a jerk of his head to the man guarding the door, and the little man said to Teresa, "Come on."

She walked proudly from the room, and when she was through the door Klaus said, "Don't let her out of your sight, Guff."

When they were gone, Klaus sat down and regarded Flood with fresh curiosity. "I was wondering for a minute, after what that floozy told me." There was no apology in his tone, only explanation. He continued bluntly, "You ain't very careful."

Flood said, "Careful enough."

"How did you know you weren't putting your proposition up to a bunch of U. S. marshals?"

"I was bluffing," Flood said frankly.

"How bluffing?"

"I figured she might try and double-cross me to save herself. When I saw you, I guessed you might be the crew Gordie worked with, so I put the proposition up to you because I had to talk first." He smiled meagerly. "If I hadn't talked first, I never would have talked, would I?"

"I reckon not," Klaus said bluntly. "Talk now."

Flood shrugged. "I told it to you straight. I can show you the stuff if you can get rid of it."

"What stuff?" Klaus asked cautiously.

Flood leaned back. "All right. Now you talk."

One of the men behind Klaus pulled a chair out and sat down. The others did the same. They kept looking at Klaus and Flood, waiting.

Klaus said finally, "What do you know about us?

Maybe I don't know what you mean."

"Maybe not," Flood said.

Klaus said, after a long wait, "You mean cattle?"

"I know when a herd is going to hit the Ruidoso. I know within three days. I can tell you how many men there will be and where they will bed down the stuff. I can even get in with them so you can place your men."

Klaus' eyes changed a little, shone a little through their sleepily suspicious dullness. He said, "What's that to us, to me?"

"I don't know," Flood said easily. "What is it?"

"How do you know all this?" Klaus asked.

"I'm supposed to join them at the river. Right now I'm supposed to be picking out a way off the trail to get a herd up into the Colorado mining camps without swinging over to the American."

"How many?" Klaus said.

"Close to three thousand."

Klaus looked fleetingly at one of the men, but his face was impassive. He said to Flood, "How did you know where to come?"

"Gordie was killed trying to rustle a trail herd down by the Point Loma badlands. There's only two towns close to them: Clearcreek and Cienega. That girl did the rest."

Klaus said, "And how do we—what you got to prove that this ain't a trap worse than the one Gordie walked into?"

"Nothing," Flood admitted. "What have I got to prove that the lot of you won't gang up on me when you know what I have to tell you?"

Klaus said gently, a little mockingly, "Why, we wouldn't do that. This would be a business deal."

"That's it. A business deal. You take care of yourself and I take care of myself," Flood said coldly.

Klaus considered him a quiet moment and said nothing.

"You take a long chance on believing me," Flood went on. "But I take a longer chance after it happens. That's fair, isn't it?"

Klaus ignored this and said softly, "It sounds good. Maybe you come to the right place."

Flood nodded.

"Understand," Klaus said, "I can't—" He paused and said quickly, "What cut do you expect out of this?"

"A third in the bank before I tell you a thing."

"That's plenty," Klaus said, after a pause.

"Two thousand cattle for you is better than none, isn't it?" Flood countered. "I'll be with you, so that if I'm lying, you'll have me. When it happens, my share will be in the bank in my name, so you won't have any reason to kill me for my money. Besides, that would be poor business, because I can likely bring other herds this way."

Klaus smiled meagerly. "You've thought this all out, ain't you?"

"It's a business deal," Flood said coldly. "We can leave out all those speeches about trusting each other, because we don't."

This time Klaus laughed, and Flood guessed it was with grudging admiration.

Flood went on carelessly, "The details I'll discuss with the man that pays you. Nobody else."

Klaus's smile vanished. "The man that pays us?" He paused, and his face got wary. "Nobody pays us, Flood. I'm the boss here, and I run this with nobody over me."

Flood only smiled tolerantly and repeated, "With the man that pays you."

Klaus said, "I say I'm the boss here." Without turning, he said to the men, "Ain't that right, boys?"

They said it was.

Flood shook his head. "That's too bad. When you come to your senses I'll talk business."

Klaus stood up, his chair scraping loudly. "You'll talk business now, mister."

"If you kill me now, you've lost a nice piece of money," Flood said calmly without getting up. "You can't get the cattle without me."

"We've got others without you," Klaus said thickly.

"And lost three men doing it."

"Not that. Another herd," Klaus growled.

Flood gave no sign that this meant anything to him, but he knew the reference was to Shifflin's herd. He said, "Maybe you aren't interested in this at all, then."

Klaus leaned over the table. "But maybe you are. You'll never get away from here knowing what you know. We'll see to that."

"Exactly," Flood said. "You say I can't leave, because you won't let me. And I won't talk to understrappers. That puts me here with information you want, and you with men enough to act on it." He smiled and shrugged. "We might as well come to an agreement now, because I don't intend to wait."

Klaus glared at him in silence. Then he said, "Why do you think I ain't boss of this outfit?"

Flood leaned across the table and spoke calmly, flatly. "I know greed when I see it, Klaus. If you had been running this, you would have taken up my proposition without a question. I could see it in your face. But you haven't said yes or no yet. You can't until you see the man that pays you." He leaned back again, then said, "You are not the man I deal with. Take me to him."

Klaus cursed him, and Flood only looked bored. Klaus ceased then and said meaningly, "What if there is a man above me and I won't take you to him? What about that?"

Flood only smiled. "You are a fool, Klaus, but not that big a fool. Four men here have heard me offer them a chance to make a nice little stake. Do you think they are going to stand by and see themselves done out of it, just because you like to bluff?"

Before Klaus had a chance to answer, Flood rose indolently from the chair. "I'll wait till morning, Klaus. If you haven't changed your mind by then, don't ever bother to change it. Take me to the man that pays you, or we'll forget all this."

"Will we?" Klaus said softly. "You seem to forget, mister, this is our town. Things happen here that don't happen other places."

Flood said calmly, "But not to me, Klaus. Have I got

to tell you again that these men won't tolerate your stubbornness when it means money to them?" He drew out his pipe and packed it, saying, "For an understrapper, you are a loyal man, Klaus. But I don't do business with understrappers." He tapped his chest with curved forefinger. "I call the turn from now on. Don't forget that. Tomorrow morning is the deadline."

And saying it, Flood knew he was forcing their hand. If the man who paid them lived over the mountains, if he was one of those men fighting for the Silver Creek range, as Flood was sure he was, then there would not be enough time to get to him with the name Flood. Either these men would take him to the man he wanted to see, or they would kill him.

He lighted his pipe, under the hot stare of Klaus.

"Is there a hotel in town?" he asked.

When nobody answered him, he said, "If there is, you can find me there. Goodnight to you."

He opened the door, his back crawling, and turned into it, and his step was unhurried. He paused in the act, glanced at the five silent men, all watching him, then he smiled a little past the pipe clenched in his teeth and closed the door behind him.

At the head of the corridor, he did not pause as he wanted to, for he knew Guff, the little man, would be watching from somewhere in the room and would note that he stopped to look for Teresa. And that was what he was doing, although he did not stop to do it, nor show it when he caught sight of her alone at a table on the far side of the room.

Flood knew without anyone telling him that Teresa was marked for death. She had betrayed herself, and they would get her. With the law in the town on the side of her enemies, she could turn to no one. She was cornered.

Half way through the crowded room, Flood caught sight of Guff dawdling over a drink at the bar. He stood so that he could see Teresa. Flood knew he must get her out of here some way, but he did not know how yet.

He idled over to the gaming tables and stood watching a faro game. He watched it without seeing it, looking up occasionally at the faces of the players and the watchers. Across the table from him was a drunken miner, who was gambling with a kind of smoldering patience that was shortening each time he lost. Beside him was a percentage girl trying vainly to get him away from the table while her interest and his money lasted. The man was sullen, unheeding, and the house man was watching him with a pitying, polite look.

Flood sized up the percentage girl with a curious quickening of his pulse. Perhaps this was what he had been waiting for. He stretched on tiptoe, watching the play, so that anyone observing him might think he was not able to see well from where he stood. Then he sank back on his heels and moved along the fringe of watchers, pausing occasionally to look at the play. He did this until he was directly behind the girl and the miner, and then he gently wedged his way through the onlookers until he was next her. Flood heard her say to the miner, "You promised the next time you lost."

The miner said nothing. Flood said from beside her, so that the miner would not hear, "He ought to quit."

The girl, a blond, big woman with a placid, thick face, turned to Flood with good-natured despair. "He's gotta lose his poke first."

Flood smiled at her and she smiled back, considering him as a possible customer she might shift her attentions to. Flood had some gold coins in his hand, and he stacked them in his fingers so they touched her arm. He said quietly, without looking at her, "Would you like to earn these?"

She looked down, while he glanced over the circle of heads opposite him to the little man, who was drinking, watching Teresa.

"Sure," the blond girl whispered.

Flood put the money in her hand. He said, "You see Teresa over there alone at that wall table?"

The girl looked and said she did.

"When your friend loses enough that he wants to

quit, take him over to her table and sit down with Teresa."

"Why?"

"Tell her to sit there until the commotion starts. When it does, tell her to get out of here and go over to the hotel and register under the name of Flood. Have you got that?"

"Yes."

"And when she has done that, tell her to go up to the room they give her."

"Is that all?"

"No. Tell her if she doubts me, to get a gun before she comes up." Flood put more coins in her hand. "With this," he said.

"All right," she answered, taking them. "What else?"

Flood handed her another stack of coins. "That's for a pair of red shoes to remind you to keep your pretty mouth shut."

The girl wasn't looking at him now, and she smiled. Flood waited a moment, then backed out and walked over to a monte table. He watched this for a while, then left it for the bar. Guff was still watching Teresa.

Flood stood up to the bar beside him, and Guff grinned impudently.

"You don't look like a cowman," Flood said dryly, "so have a drink with me."

"I can't find a poker game, so I don't mind if I do."

Flood smiled. He was looking in the bar mirror, sizing up the men drinking. It was getting late now, and the noise of the room was louder as men began to feel the evening's drinks. Flood picked out his man, a big, bluff, red-faced miner in high boots and a wet hat, who was drinking Gargantuan slugs of whisky from a water glass. He picked out a second and a third possibility, all big men, all well into drink. When the blond girl crossed with her man to Teresa's table Guff was saying, "What I can't figure out is, who believed who about that poker game."

Flood said, "That's a poor way to meet a man—by spilling his drink. Some day you'll get your teeth knocked down your throat before you get a chance to apologize."

Guff chuckled, but Flood was watching the red-faced drinker in the bar mirror.

Guff said, "I think you wanted to come."

"I was waiting for you, or someone like you."

He saw the red-faced man turn away from the bar and survey the room. The man said something to his companion Flood did not catch, and then started toward the gaming tables. To get there, he had to skirt the men at the bar. Flood watched him in the mirror until he was almost even with him, then he turned sideways to the bar and crossed his legs exaggeratedly. He timed it perfectly. His foot knifed into the big man's heavy walk. There was a quick tangle of feet, and the miner crashed to the floor.

Flood set down his drink as the miner rolled into a sitting position.

"You take a lot of room to get around," Flood drawled with open good humor.

The miner struggled to his feet, his face flushed angrily.

"You done that a-purpose," he growled, and his voice was thick with whisky.

"You're drunk," Flood said, smiling, his tone nicely calculated to goad the miner. The men at the bar were watching.

The miner was a man of few words. He stepped toward Flood, drawing back his arm. Flood dived toward him, slammed up against him, his hands reaching and pinning the miner's arms to his side. Then the wrestle began, a grunting, heaving thrashing that cleared a circle for them in a few seconds. The man was as powerful as a bull, and fought much like one, with his head down, his feet digging for a foothold, but his arms pinned to his side by the clinging Flood. Quickly the crowd in the room, women in the fore, milled toward the fight, and in a moment Flood saw he was surrounded by a circle of laughing, curious faces. Guff, he noted, too, was on the inside of the circle, struggling ineffectually to work his way out.

Flood shoved the miner from him, backing away himself. "Take it easy, pardner," he said good-humoredly. "You're too drunk to put up a scrap."

"Damned if he ain't," a watcher observed, getting a laugh.

But the miner came in again, and again Flood caught his arms and pinned them, so that he rode the force of the miner's slugging with the whole dragging weight of his body. People began to laugh now, watching the fight. Flood shoved him away again and stood breathing a little hard, smiling.

He said, "Take a breather and I'll buy you a drink."

Suddenly the miner, a good-natured man himself, saw the humor in the situation. He grinned.

"Sure."

Flood took his arm and they stepped over to the bar. The crowd broke up, laughing, and Flood ordered the drinks. They both had to pause a moment to get their breaths, and in that time Flood glanced casually toward the table where Teresa was sitting. She was gone.

He also had a glimpse of Guff elbowing his slow way through the returning drinkers toward the back corridor. He looked at the miner, who smiled and raised his glass. Flood drank with him, and said, "Maybe I belong on a horse, after all," smiling a little as he said it.

The miner laughed. "Reckon I've been muckin' around too many test pits to watch my step."

They shook hands, and the miner resumed his way to the tables. Flood waited a moment, knowing the bartender might be watching him, and when, a minute later, nobody spoke to him and the bar resumed its business, he paid for the drinks and left.

Out in the night, he stopped a man and inquired where the hotel was, and then followed the directions that took him across the street, through the slow rain and the deep mud, to a square building several doors down.

At the hotel desk he inquired of an old man if anyone named Flood was registered here.

The old man nodded. "First name's Mark. Never heard tell of a woman with that name. Don't believe it."

Flood got the room number on the second floor back and climbed the stairs. When he came to the right number, he noticed that a pencil of light gleamed under the door. He knocked.

"Come," a voice said. Flood paused only a split second, then he swept the door open.

Margot was standing by the bed, straight, her lips parted a little.

"Darling, I could not wait for you," she said softly.

CHAPTER EIGHTEEN

MARGOT HAD PROMISED HERSELF she would not burden Flood with her troubles until this thing of his that she could not name or guess at was settled. And in his arms she found the strength she knew she would find to keep her resolve. All the tight, bitter grief of these last two days was dissolving, and the courage and power of him seemed to flow through her at his touch.

He did not speak for a long while, and then he led her to the bed.

"How did you find me?" he asked gently.

"Through the notch, where you said you were going. I saw your horse at the stable and knew you must come here eventually."

"Has anything happened?"

Then Margot told him of Lee's murder. "There was nothing left for me, Mark. My place is with you. I had to come. Do you see it?" she finished.

Flood nodded slowly, but there was a reserve in him that frightened her.

"Mark, is it all right? I don't mind if you are a hunted man over there. I just want to be with you—die with you if I have to."

He smiled away the concern in her eyes, and sat down on the bed beside her.

"Who was it that killed Lee?"

"Mark," she said gently, disregarding his question, "is it all right?"

"Yes, except that I meant never to have you share this trouble with me. I wanted to come to you free, all of me, not just the part that I didn't need to win through this."

"But I want to help you, Mark. I have enough of you now." But she shook her head now, contradicting herself. "No. That part is true enough; but I wanted to be the kind of woman who would not possess you, no matter how much I wanted to, because you would not tolerate that. I can see I'm doing that now."

Flood's swift, almost fierce look met hers. "I want you to possess me that way. I want you to have all there is of me, but you can't now. There is this thing." He stood up and walked slowly around the end of the bed, then stopped and looked at Margot.

"Do you know who killed Lee?" he asked again.

When Margot said no, he said, "Do you believe it could have been Petrie? Did he see you come to me?"

She knew now that it had come, and that this secret she and Lee had kept all this while must be kept still longer from him as it had from Honeywell, but not for the same reason. She said, "No. I could never believe he could do that, Mark."

Flood looked deep into her eyes, and he said quietly, "You know why he was killed, then?"

She rose and came over to him and laid her hands on his shoulders. "I will not lie, Mark. I do know. I do not know who killed him, though. But you must not ask me more. That part of me died with Lee, and this must, too. But you will know, too, some time."

She wanted to know if he understood she was trying to spare him, and if he did, she knew it would be intolerable for him. But the question in his eyes had melted into that sleepy reserve that held no curiosity, only patience, and his still dark face was unreadable. She could never know now.

A movement behind him drew her attention. The

door was inching open. She said in a whisper, "The door, Mark."

He whirled, his body shielding her, his hand on the grip of his gun.

"Come in, Teresa," he said, and let his hand drop.

Teresa stepped inside the door, a gun held before her, which beaded Flood with steady menace. She shut the door behind her and leaned against it.

"I will take you with me, anyway," she said coldly. "That is all I want."

Flood stepped aside and said, "Teresa, this is Miss Curtin."

Margot murmured something, but Teresa's cold glance swept Margot and left her for Flood, and her taut face did not change expression.

Flood said, "Did he follow you?"

"Why should he? I'm here, where he wants me. You even fixed it so that all Brothers would have to do would be to look out his window and see me come."

"He didn't, though?" Flood asked quickly.

Teresa laughed softly. "No. I came in the back way. I wanted to be sure I got as far as here, where you would be."

Flood said, "Do you think I got you out of that saloon to lead you into a trap?"

"Yes," Teresa said flatly.

Margot stood motionless.

Flood said, "You've got to get out of here. They will kill you."

"Yes, here or outside. It doesn't matter much, except that now you'll go, too."

"Are you quiet enough to listen to me before you shoot?" Flood asked, not moving.

"Yes. That's why I came, partly—to see you squirm," Teresa said.

"Then get away from that door," Flood said; and when she did not move he said, "If anyone is out there, as you think, they can shoot through that door and kill you before you can move."

Teresa considered this, and Flood breathed more

easily when she walked across the room to another wall.
At least she was reasonable.

He said, "Margot, go over and sit down."

Margot looked at him, but he was watching Teresa.
She went over and sat down, numb with fear.

Then Flood said, "That was a fool trick to come to
me in the barroom this afternoon. They knew you were
Gordie's woman. They knew my name. If I hadn't
goaded you into slapping me, we might both be dead
now."

Teresa said, "Squirm," smiling.

Flood thought a moment, his scowl deepening the
creases of his face. Then he said, "All right, maybe you
can understand this: Ten men have died since Gordie
did. Killed by the same man. Can you understand that?"

"What of it?"

"That's why I'm here," Flood said. "To lie and fight
and bluff my way into the confidence of these men, so
that I can find the man who guides all this. Then Gordie's debt will be settled, along with theirs."

"So you betrayed me to Klaus, because I offered to
take you to men you wanted to get in with?" Teresa said
mockingly.

"I told you why I refused you there in the barroom.
You told me these men were killers, and that they had
deserted Gordie. Word was sure to get to them that we
had been seen together, because I gave my name at the
bar. How would it have looked to them if we talked
alone and parted friends?"

She did not believe him, Flood saw, but she was listening. So he told her, talking to Margot now, too, how
the trail herd under Shifflin had disappeared at the
Ruidoso; how he had been accused by Wheat of plotting
this steal with the same men Gordie had run with; how
he had backed away from them, gun in hand, to settle
this for himself and to avenge these deaths; how he did
not know until Teresa told him that Gordie had been
left to die while these men escaped with the Munro
herd; and how he believed that if he could find these
men Gordie had run with, he would have the men who

had stolen Shifflin's herd. And he talked slowly, patiently, logically, because he knew he was talking for his life
now.

And when he was finished with that he did not pause,
but he jumped immediately to what had passed this
evening, and as he talked, Margot saw a change come
over Teresa, and she began to tremble violently, because
she had not realized how afraid she had been.

Mark was saying, "When I walked into that room
with Klaus, I knew that you had betrayed me. My only
chance was to betray you, and do it innocently, pretend-
ing I believed they were gathered there to listen to my
plans for stealing another trail herd. I couldn't let them
believe you, or I was gone, and all your hope of aveng-
ing Gordie would be gone, too."

He paused, studying her, and he knew now that his
story was finding credence with her, but he did not stop.

"When I left the room I knew what they would do
with you. I knew, because they sent Guff to watch you,
and because there is no one in this place that could
protect you. I knew if you were to live, that I would
have to get you out of there and then out of the country.
That's why my message was sent by the girl and her
miner, because if I was discovered trying to help you,
all my talking would not have saved either of us." He
paused. "That is why I am going to take you out of the
country tonight."

The anger and defiance had washed out of Teresa's
face, and she was staring at Flood with a curious, almost
shy, look. Now, for the first time, she looked at Margot,
and then back at Flood.

"I—I guess I'm soft," she said harshly. "It sounds like
you meant it."

"I do. Now put your gun up, Teresa."

"Not yet," Teresa said doggedly. She was silent for a
moment, trying to pick flaws in what Flood had told
her. Suddenly she said, "A word from you, a note or
anything, would have kept me from telling Klaus.
Didn't you think of that?"

"How would I have got it to you?" Flood asked.

"Who could I trust in this whole town?" He shook his head. "The stakes were too high to risk it, Teresa. I went back to the saloon, hoping I could send you a word-of-mouth message by one of the percentage girls. I couldn't put it in writing, and I couldn't be seen talking to you."

"And have you made a deal with Klaus and his men?" Teresa asked curiously.

"I think so. I will know by tomorrow morning. I refused to bargain with anybody but the man who pays them." He said slowly, "You don't know who he is, do you, Teresa?"

"Do you think he'd be alive if I did?" Teresa countered.

"No, I don't. Now put up your gun."

Teresa slowly laid her gun on the table and said gently, "This will be the second time I have trusted a Flood." She smiled crookedly. "You see, I can't help it."

Margot rose and went over to her. "Believe me, he will help you," she said simply.

Teresa looked up at her. "Who are you?" she asked quietly.

"It doesn't matter," Margot said. "I love him, like you loved Gordie."

Teresa nodded, and Margot turned away from her to Flood.

"Is this what it is, Mark? Is this what must be settled before we can be free?"

Flood nodded. "My name is pretty black now with some men. It was my idea to make up the trail herd in Texas. I was trail boss. I owe it to all these men, the living and the dead."

"But are you sure, Mark, that these men Gordie ran with, the men that stole the Munro herd, are the same men that stole yours?"

"They let that much slip tonight," Flood said.

"And would this same man whose name you want be the one who directed both steals?"

There was pain in Flood's eyes, but he answered, "I think so."

Margot said then, "I should never have come, should I?"

Flood said, "I am going to send you away." He spoke to Teresa. "You will go together."

Teresa smiled sadly. "You don't know what you are saying. Right now they are hunting the town for me. I can't escape."

Flood looked at Margot. "Will you take her home—to Clearcreek?"

"Yes, if you say so," Margot answered.

Flood was watching her, and his face was drawn with worry, but he knew there was no going back now. Margot had made her bargain to share this with him, and it was a step that he hated. But she had chosen it because of him, and he knew he must let her share the danger, because she would not have it any other way. To protect her would mean that he counted her help nothing. Both knew and understood without saying it. Flood gripped her shoulder tightly, and a beginning smile broke his grave face.

"Yes," he said. He went over to Teresa now and sat on the edge of the table.

"You'll get out," he said. "Tell me about the town now. Where does the road north go?"

To the mines far up the valley, then it split into several trails that took to the peaks, and were used only by prospectors and mountain men, she told him.

"But from there on?" Flood asked. "Do the trails disappear, or do they join other trails that will put a man into different country over west?"

Teresa thought a minute and said yes, that she had heard of men coming through over high, windswept passes, and that these men had been weeks doing it, but that she had heard them speak of a desert country from where they started.

Flood said, "Then there is a way over them? You know that? You've talked to the men who have done it?"

Teresa said yes, and Flood looked questioningly over to Margot.

"I can do it, Mark," Margot said quietly, in answer

to his unspoken question. "I tracked you across the pass from Silver Creek. I can make it west if you say."

Flood shook his head. "That's not the way we'll do it. You and Teresa will go back to Clearcreek across the mountains." He paused, regarding her anxiously. "You'll have to camp in the rain without a fire, and you'll be wet and cold and hungry, and you won't sleep. You'll leave in an hour or so, and you'll travel up this mountain tonight in the dark and rain. You'll reach the top by daylight, and from then on you'll have to hurry, because I'll be close behind you. When you reach the Silver Creek range, you'll pull off and hide until you see me ride by. I'll be with another man, I think. Then you can come into town behind us. Can you do all that?"

"If you can get us out of town," Margot said.

Flood said quietly, "I'm sharing it with you, Margot."

"That was my bargain, Mark."

Flood took his hat and went to the door. "Make two bedrolls from the blankets on the bed, and be ready."

And then he was gone.

CHAPTER NINETEEN

In life, Breckenridge was as hard with horses as he was with men, so that in death his horse did not ignore the trailing reins until along toward night, when he got both hungry and thirsty.

Darkness found him wandered back along the trail to the pasture between the two ridges. He fed there through the night, fretting only a little at the bit in his mouth and saddle on his back. By the next morning there was enough dew on the grass to quiet his thirst, so he continued to graze there through the morning until the heat of midday made him thirsty. He started moving then and was around the end of the first ridge when a rider picked him up.

The rider was one of those who had followed Coe in

the stampede, and he regarded the saddled, ground-haltered horse with some reflection. He knew it was Breck's horse, and the horse was ground-haltered, but still it was walking. The trailing reins had been scarred and cut, and were wet with grass stain. A few inches of one rein had been tromped off, all of which argued the horse had been riderless for some time.

Like many of his companions of that night who had joined Coe out of spite and bravado, this man had been a little appalled at what he had helped do. At the coming of the Wagon Hammer riders, these men had scattered and slunk home, and were wondering now with a kind of craven fear if their names were known. This man had been to Clearcreek most of the day, just listening to talk. With much patience, he had discovered that the names of the men with Coe were not known. He was still uneasy, however, so when he saw Breck's horse, he had an idea.

What could be more obliging and natural, more indicative of a man with an open nature and nothing to hide, than to ride over to the Wagon Hammer with this horse? He would do it. In his eagerness, not once did he pause to wonder what had happened to Breckenridge.

As he expected, the man found most of the Wagon Hammer riders in. The house itself was a two-story log affair at the foot of a long grassy slope, so that he was seen long before he reached it. A cluster of scrub oak fringed the stream by the house, while the corrals and outbuildings lay on the other side of the place. An addition of newly peeled logs joined the house on the corral side, and the man guessed this was the new office he heard Petrie had added to the house.

A half dozen men walked out from the bunkhouse to meet him, and he handed over Breckenridge's horse to them with the observation that he looked like he needed water.

Petrie came out of the office now and walked over to him.

"Where'd you find him?" Petrie asked.

The man told him. "It's Breck's pony, ain't it?"

Petrie nodded curtly, regarding the pony with a kind of irritable curiosity. His face was surly, unshaven, and the bandage he wore on his cheek was dirty. Evidently, he had been sleeping after the trip back from town, where he had been most of the morning. His hair was mussed, his eyes red and sleepy, and his usual confidence had turned into a sultry arrogance of manner. There was not a mark on his face from his battle with Flood.

"You didn't see Breck, did you?"

The man shook his head. Petrie told four of his men to saddle up, and then he addressed the man again. "Show me the spot where you picked him up, will you?"

The rider paused to consider before he answered, for he wanted it to appear as if he were making something of a concession with his time. Then he agreed, and did not wonder at the fact that he got no thanks for it. Along with Petrie and four riders, he returned to where he had picked up the horse. When the direction from which Breck's horse had come was established, it was evident that he had wandered down this long valley. Once in the pasture between the two ridges, Petrie directed one man to go up the trail a way for signs, the others to wait until he returned. As soon as the Wagon Hammer hand had reached the trail, he turned and rode back with the announcement that the horse had traveled from that direction, since the dragging reins had left their mark in the dust.

Ten minutes later they rode on to Breck's body. All dismounted except Petrie, who sat his horse with a faint look of disgust on his face. The verdict of the men examining Breck's body was so obvious that he smiled sardonically.

"Shot in the chest, eh?" he murmured. "All right. Who shot him?"

None of the men said anything, and Petrie looked around him with careless indifference at the hills. Then he looked at them again and said sharply, "Don't blot those tracks. Look around you."

He didn't comment when one of the men announced that there were tracks going west made about the same time as those of Breck's horse.

"That wouldn't be you, then?" Petrie said to the man who had brought in the horse. He only laughed at the man's discomfort and said to his men, "Two of you go home for a wagon. I'm going into town."

He rode slowly back to the pasture and crossed the ridge and angled down the hillside past the cemetery. On the ride, he rolled a half dozen cigarettes and threw them away as soon as he had taken a few puffs. His every gesture was marked with a taut, savage disgust.

Only at the edge of town did he remember that nobody was with him, and then he knew why his men had looked so strangely at him when he announced where he was going. He went on, anyway.

He saw Honeywell on the street, and Sam waved glumly to him without giving him much notice. At the bank, a narrow little cubbyhole with a cracked window, he dismounted and entered.

"How much cash—gold—have you got on hand?" he asked the single clerk, an obsequious little man in shirtsleeves.

"I'd have to count it, Mr. Petrie."

"Go ahead."

"Uh—are you thinking of making a large withdrawal?"

"Why do you think I asked?" Petrie inquired surlily.

"Yes, sir."

He smoked two cigarettes while the clerk went back to the small safe in the rear and busied himself.

When the clerk returned, he said, "A little over six thousand in currency."

"Give me five of it," Petrie said. "Put it in canvas sacks."

"I'm afraid I'll have to get Mr. Sewell's consent to that," the clerk said apologetically. "That will leave us pretty short, Mr. Petrie."

"Go get it, then," Petrie said shortly.

He stepped out and walked down to Sewell's store, the clerk following a few steps behind him. He paid no attention when the clerk walked through the store and

up the stairs to Sewell's office. At the counter he asked
for saddlebags and paid for them. By this time Sewell
had come down the stairs and approached him.

Petrie said, without turning to the banker, "I'm not
fooling, Frank. I want five thousand cash tonight."

Sewell was the counterpart of his clerk, only a score
of years older.

"But what if this starts a run, Petrie? We can't handle
it."

Petrie said, "I've got more than twice that amount
in your bank, Frank. I want it now."

"But think what will happen."

Petrie turned on him, eyes blazing. "What kind of a
damn do I give what happens! It's my money, and I
want it. If I don't get it I'll demand all of it. Take your
choice."

Sewell backed off and conferred with the clerk, who
went out again.

When Petrie returned to the bank, the clerk was
filling two canvas sacks with gold pieces. Finished, he
gave them to Petrie with a slip to sign. He watched
Petrie put the gold in the saddlebags and walk out, and
he cursed feebly, but none the less bitterly, at his back.

Petrie adjusted the saddlebags, and this time rode out
of town west and up the hill. His pace was leisurely.
Once, just as it was getting dusk, he stopped and dismounted and tied the drawstrings tighter on one of the
sacks, so that the money would not rattle. He also stuffed
the saddlebags full of grass, which served as a packing
for the canvas sacks.

It was after dark when he reached Hartley's. Hartley
stood in the door of his shack with a lantern, and he
said not a word when Petrie pulled up his horse.

"Going to ask me in, Phil?" Petrie inquired dryly.

"Get down."

Petrie dismounted and left his horse ground-haltered
and entered the cabin. He threw himself down in a
chair while Hartley set the lamp on the table.

"I'm looking for Emory," Petrie said dully, rubbing
a hand over his face.

"I'm not in this, Loosh. Don't look for him here," Hartley said flatly, and added, "You alone?"

Petrie nodded. "I found Breck dead today," he said calmly.

Hartley didn't speak for a moment, then observed, "You might of expected that, considerin'."

"I know," Petrie said wearily. "I'm whipped, Phil. Range cleaned, men dead. And what have I got out of it?"

"Coe dead, Morgan dead, young Curtin dead—I dunno whether that's part of this or not, but he's dead—Breck dead, Kenney dead and seven others over on your side of the range. That's what you got out of it," Hartley said implacably.

Petrie waved a hand in protest. "I know. I know. I want to get word to Hand to call this off. Where is he?"

"I don't know," Hartley said. "I don't even want to know."

"I thought that's the way it would be. That's why I want to talk to Emory. Where's he?"

"Up at the Brush Creek line camp, I reckon."

"How can I get word to him? If I rode up there I'd get cut to doll rags before I could open my mouth."

Hartley regarded him with cautious speculation. "This don't sound much like you, Loosh."

Petrie smiled wryly. He spread one of his hands out on the table and gazed at it abstractedly. "This is a weary range, Phil," he said slowly. "Bled out. All I ever owned I've lost. I want to call it off while I've still got a roof over me."

"What about that Silver Creek range?"

Petrie looked up at him and smiled wryly. "You don't have any use for grass if you haven't got the cattle to eat it, do you?"

Hartley considered him a minute, then he said, "I'll take you up to Emory. Want to eat first?"

"I couldn't."

Hartley went out to the corral, saddled his horse, and they rode off in the night toward the mountains. It was a silent ride. They took the same route Flood and Hand had taken the first night.

When they were in sight of the line shack, Hartley said, "You better hang back till I tell them about this."

"All right. I don't know who's there, Phil. If Hand is, I want to talk to him alone. If he isn't there and Emory is, I want to talk to him alone. Or Flood. Only if Flood is there, I want you to be with me."

"Don't trust him, eh?"

"He rides a little too proud to suit me. I'd kill him, sick as I am."

"Loosh, you heave that gun of yours off," Hartley warned him.

"I will."

When Hartley rode ahead, Petrie sat his horse in quiet patience. He was thinking of what he was going to tell Emory, and he smiled cynically when he thought of it. Hartley's halloo came to him in a minute and he unstrapped his gun belt and slung it over the horn, then rode on to the shack.

He approached it on the dark side, and dismounted some distance from it, tied his horse to a branch of a piñon tree and walked on.

Hartley was standing in the door, and he looked to see if Petrie had taken his gun off, then he stepped aside.

Emory and Nosey were standing by the table, on which a lantern burned. They were unshaven, tired, and they regarded Petrie with a surly truculence.

"Hand isn't here?" Petrie said to Hartley.

Nosey laughed unpleasantly, nothing more.

"Then I'll have to do business with you," Petrie said to Emory. Hand's foreman nodded, but his eyes were alert now, wary. To Hartley, Petrie said, "I want to talk to him alone. You can search me for a gun or a knife."

"I'll take your word for it," Hartley said.

"I won't," Nosey put in. He walked over to Petrie and slapped his pockets, his shirt, even looked in the tops of his boots. Petrie submitted to it, a quiet smile on his face, but when Nosey was finished he said to Hartley. "Maybe you better do the same to Emory."

Hartley's search of Emory revealed nothing except a pocket knife, which he kept. Then he said, "Come on, Nosey."

Nosey said, "I hear one yeep in here, Petrie, and I won't ask questions." He picked up a carbine standing in the corner and went out, followed by Hartley, who closed the door behind him.

Petrie was immediately at his ease. He rolled a smoke and offered his sack to Emory, who refused it, then motioned him to a chair. "Sit down, Wes. This will take some time."

They both drew chairs up to the table, Emory with a kind of stiff and hostile suspicion. There was a look of utter discouragement in his lean face, and he moved listlessly. In his dark eyes, however, lurked a hint of suspicion and curiosity. His clothes were untidy and soiled, as if he had slept in them, and he needed a shave. He toyed with a match, revolving it in his fingers and watching Petrie.

Having spoken, Petrie waited, and there seemed to return to him some of his confidence and arrogance that he had discarded while talking with Hartley.

Finally, after an uncomfortable silence, Emory said, "Get it over with."

"Get what over?"

"Hartley said you wanted to see Ben. He said you wanted to call this fight off."

"What do you think?" Petrie asked carelessly.

Emory said slowly, "I don't think you meant it."

Petrie's laugh was easy, unforced, as he leaned both arms on the table. "What are you going to do now, Wes, since you've lost your job?"

"I didn't know I'd lost it," Emory replied carefully.

Petrie shrugged. "Hand is wanted for murder. He's through in this country, after what he put Coe up to. Do you think even if that murder charge was dropped that Hand would dare come back to the Bar Stirrup and run it?"

"Flood did that," Emory said. "You hate Ben, Petrie, but you know he wasn't to blame for that."

"Maybe I do," Petrie said, "but you'll have a hard time making the widows and families and friends and relatives of those seven dead men believe that." When Emory said nothing, Petrie added, "Hand is through, Emory. He won't live a week if he comes back here. He'll stand about a month of this hiding out, and then maybe he'll try to come back. He'll face a murder charge and a lynching—if I have to breed the lynching myself. Understand that?"

"I understood it long ago," Emory sneered.

Petrie nodded and smiled. "All right, there's one thing for Hand to do. He'll have you get rid of his land and stock and he'll pull out. Where'll you be then?"

"I know cattle. I can find work."

"Exactly," Petrie said. He said in a pleasant voice, "Did you hear that Breck was bushwhacked?"

The surprise in Emory's face was genuine, but he did not speak for a moment. He regarded Petrie suspiciously, then shook his head. "No use, Petrie. I won't work for the Wagon Hammer, if that's what you're offering me."

"I thought not," Petrie said softly. "Who killed Breck, Emory?"

"I don't know. If I'd been given the chance, I would have."

"His gun was still in its holster. Whoever shot him didn't give him a warning or a chance. They just shot him."

"How much of a chance did you give Morgan when you rode him down?" Emory countered grimly.

"He had a gun. He knew his risk. He shot at us, and we got him. It was a killing, but it was an open one, almost necessary."

"Maybe Breck's killing was necessary. I never knew you to draw the line between a murder and a fight until now, Petrie."

"Hand killed him," Petrie said bluntly, slowly, smiling a little. "There was somebody riding with Breck when it happened, so Hand got out in a hurry. He had to. We don't know the man that was riding with Breck, and we never will, because that man is probably afraid to give himself up and lay himself open to the charge of murder. He ran. He didn't even bother to look for Breck's killer. He probably pulled off into cover when he saw Breck blown out of the saddle, and then he ran because he was afraid he'd get the same thing. And after he'd run a little ways, he probably got to thinking that he'd better run some more and keep out of this. That's logical, isn't it?"

Emory said, "I don't think Ben killed him."

"Hand was in a sort of hurry, too," Petrie went on, ignoring him. "But he wasn't in such a hurry that he forgot to leave something behind him that would throw the blame on another man."

"How did you know it was Hand?" Emory said quickly.

"A man in a hurry, a scared man, is apt to leave tracks. His own and his horse's. Hand did. But he left something else, I say."

"What?"

Petrie paused now, so that what he was about to say would have more effect. He pursed his lips, brushed his hand slowly over the table top, watching Emory. Then he said pleasantly, slowly, leaning forward, "A bone-handled skinning knife, Wes. Maybe you remember it. The handle is made of elk horn that was shaped by a rasp, a blacksmith's rasp. Maybe you remember the day it was done at Dave Wolff's. If you don't I can think of six or eight men who watched Dave shape it and fit it to the steel."

Emory half rose out of his chair and his tired face came to life. "That's a damned lie! That's my knife, all right, but Ben Hand would never leave it there to put the blame on me! I don't know much about men, but I know Ben wouldn't do that!"

Petrie shrugged. "It could have slipped out of the sheath when he hurried away. I don't think so, though."

"Where is the knife?" Emory asked suddenly.

Petrie smiled sardonically. "Do you think I'm damn fool enough to bring it with me, so you could murder me for it? No, that knife is safe. It will get me what I want."

Emory sat down, breathing hard, and his eyes had narrowed. "I left that knife at the Bar Stirrup days ago, before it was burned. Whoever burned the house got the knife for you to use at a time like this. Isn't that it?"

"That is not it," Petrie said flatly. "You can think that if you want, Emory. I don't care. You can believe Hand planted that knife there to throw the blame on you, like I know he did, or you can think we're trying to put Breck's murder on to you. You can believe either way. I don't care. The point is, we've got the knife. Can you understand that?"

Emory's eyes were harried now. He said softly, "What is it you want?"

"Ah," Petrie said, sitting erect. "That's more like it. You'll listen to reason now, eh?"

"What is it you want?"

Petrie slouched down comfortably and stared at Emory, a look of mild curiosity on his face. "The way I see it, Emory, there's nothing left here for you. You've risked your neck for Ben Hand and he double-crossed you by putting a murder on your head. He—"

"I say he didn't!" Emory said, pounding the table.

Petrie drawled, "You poor damn fool. Why would Hand be carrying a skinning knife? What was he going to kill and skin? He comes to you every day for his food. He isn't in the mountains so he could hunt—or is he?"

Emory thought a minute and said no.

"Then why would he have your knife if he wasn't planning to leave it by Breck—or by me, when he murdered us?" When Emory said nothing, Petrie said, "He planned to come back, Wes. He planned to kill me and Breck, and throw the blame for it on you, just like he ordered Coe to kill my friends and stampede my cattle and throw the blame on Flood. He'll stand on your necks to come back here and be top of the heap."

"What is it you want?" Emory said warily.

Again Petrie smiled. "I'll begin again. I said there was nothing left for you here, after this. How would you like to ride out of this country with enough gold to buy yourself a neat little outfit and stock it and be independent the rest of your life?"

Emory said slowly, "I'd like it, who wouldn't?"

"Who wouldn't?" Petrie echoed.

Emory said, "What's the rest of it?"

"The rest of it," Petrie said casually, "is that you tell me where Ben Hand is now." Before Emory could answer, Petrie said sharply, "He crossed you. He sold you out so he could come back here and king it over this range. He gave Coe orders to kill innocent men and blamed it on Flood. He's dirty and crooked and cunning as hell, Wes. God knows, you've been loyal enough to him. You don't owe him more. You've fought his fights and bled for him and now this war is on your shoulders."

And now he pointed a finger at Emory and said quietly, "If you don't want to tell, Wes, that's all right with me. I'll turn in the knife to Mayhew, and I'll bring witnesses to swear where I found it. Then everything will happen like Ben Hand wants it to. You'll hang and he'll start gunning for me. He'll likely do to Nosey or Hartley what he did to you. He'll murder me and he'll hang it on them. And that's what your loyalty will get you."

Emory was listening, his mouth a straight, bloodless line. Petrie said easily, "Tell me where he is and you ride out of here a rich man. Don't tell me, and you'll swing. And while you are swinging, you'll remember that you are doing it so Ben Hand goes free."

Emory got up and walked over to a bunk and sat on it, his face in hands. Suddenly, he stood up and walked over to the table and said in a choked voice, "I don't think you've got the knife, Petrie."

"Have you got it?" Petrie countered swiftly.

"No. I told you where I left it. But I think you are bluffing."

Petrie said softly, sardonically, "You don't think it enough to risk your neck on it, do you?"

Emory's gaze was beaten down. He dropped into his

chair and sat there peacefully, staring at the table top. Presently he said, "If I only knew you had it. If I could only believe you."

Petrie stood up. "All right, Wes. If I've got to hang you to prove I have the knife, I'll do it. And when you are in jail, just wait for Hand to come around and tell how the knife got there by Breck. Just wait."

Emory stood up, his face haggard. "For God's sake, sit down, Loosh. Don't go!"

Petrie sat down carelessly. "There's a limit to loyalty, Wes. Do you have to be killed to find that out?"

Emory rubbed a hand over his face and stared at Petrie, who wisely kept silent.

"How much money have you here?"

"Five thousand dollars. You'll admit that's pretty generous."

Emory said in a husky voice, "I've got to take a lot for granted, Petrie. I don't know whether Breck is dead. I—"

"Ask Hartley," Petrie put in. "Ask Mayhew. Ask any Wagon Hammer man."

"All right, but I don't know if Ben's tracks were near Breck. I—"

"I'll show you his tracks. Who else would kill Breck if Hand didn't? You didn't. Nosey didn't. Flood wouldn't. He's through with this row. Would your friends? No, not without Hand to back them up, and he's gone."

"All right. But I haven't seen the knife—"

"And won't. Not until Mayhew shows it to you when he arrests you."

Emory gave up. He sat down and stared vacantly at Petrie and Petrie was quick to take advantage. His tone was businesslike now.

"I can show you the knife and the tracks if you like. We'll ride down now and see them. But if I do that, you'll get only twenty-five hundred dollars from me."

"Why only half?" Emory asked.

"Because Nosey might follow us, or Hartley. He'd think it would look queer. He might warn Hand to change his hide-out, and all this would be wasted. If you take me there now, the five thousand is yours."

He was counting on Emory's greed, and he counted rightly, for he had won and he knew it.

"You say you've got the five thousand out in your saddlebags?"

"Yes."

Emory said wretchedly, "A man has got to live, hasn't he? He can't trust anything in this world but money."

Petrie said nothing.

"All right," Emory said wearily, rising. "Let's go."

Petrie rose quickly. "Good. Call Nosey in here and tell him you are taking me to Hand for a parley. Insist that you go alone. Tell him you aren't sure of me yet, and that you want a rifle. Tell him he's got to stay here in case this is just a trick to draw you away while I raid the place and your cattle too. Tell him to convince Hartley he must stay too."

"You've thought this all out, haven't you?" Emory said, quietly bitter.

"I'm a careful man," Petrie said grimly.

Without another word, Emory walked to the door and stepped outside. Petrie heard him conferring with Nosey. Presently, he came to the door.

"I'm ready," he said.

As they stepped outside, Hartley's quiet voice said to Petrie, "This is one thing you'll never forget, Loosh. Go through with it, no matter what it costs you."

"It's costing me plenty," Petrie said dryly, then, as if he did not wish to be misunderstood, he said, "I've learned a lesson, Phil."

When they had ridden away south from the cabin Emory pulled his horse up, and said, "Let's see the money."

Petrie pulled up too, and his voice was perfectly sure, perfectly calm, as he told him, "You'll get half now. You'll tell me the place where Hand is hiding too. Then you'll get the rest after it's done."

"I won't help kill him!" Emory said hotly, and his voice was full of shame.

"No. I'll do that. Tell me where he is."

"Damn you! Damn you!" Emory cursed miserably, impotently.

"The place," Petrie reminded him coldly.

Emory sighed shudderingly. "You remember that sandstone outcrop on the mesa wall on the north side of the Silver Creek range?"

"The red or brown sandstone?"

"The red."

"All right."

"There's a big cave back in the stuff. Ever been back in it?"

"Twice, I think."

"Do you know where that pinnacle rock is that looks like a big Indian drum?"

"Yes."

"The cave is half way up the wall closest to that rock, about a hundred yards north."

Without commenting, Petrie turned around and took one sack of gold from the saddlebag and handed it to Emory. He watched, a sardonic smile on his lean face, while Emory struck a match in haste and fumbled at the drawstring of the sack. The match went out and Emory cursed and then struck another. Holding it and the sack in one hand against the saddle horn, he rammed his hand deep into the gold coins. He drew a long, shuddering breath then and stilled his fingers.

"Wait till I tie this," he mumbled.

Petrie said nothing, waiting. Emory carried the sack now, and no matter how he held it, the coins jingled faintly with the motion of the horse. They had ridden for perhaps a half hour when Emory pulled up and said viciously, "Can't I stop that damned noise?"

Petrie chuckled. "Put it in my bags and stuff them with grass."

Emory only spurred his horse and rode on ahead. Petrie knew something was brewing, and he had an idea what it was, but he kept silent. When they reached the top of the mesa and were in open country, Emory dropped back beside him. The coins were still jingling faintly.

"When did Hand kill Breck?" Emory asked.

Petrie thought a moment, and said carelessly, "The tracks showed about yesterday afternoon."

"Are you sure about that?" Emory asked in a tight voice.

Petrie's hand dropped to his gun, and he sneaked it out of the holster, holding it along his pony's flank.

"Yes, why?"

Emory stopped now. "Then it's a damned lie! I spent all yesterday afternoon with Ben!"

Petrie raised his gun and shot twice. At that distance, even in the night, he could not have missed. The only sound he got on the backwash of the shot was the grunt Emory gave as his body hit the ground.

Petrie edged his horse close to Emory's, which had shied, and seized the bridle. Immediately the pony became docile and Petrie dismounted. It took very little time to untie Emory's slicker from behind the cantle and spread it over Emory's saddle seat. Then Petrie went over to Emory, struck a match and observed him for a short moment.

Satisfied, he picked up the bag of coins and put them in his saddlebag again, stuffing it with grass to kill any noise. Then he went over to Emory, picked him up and slung him face down across his saddle, and tied him there with his own lariat. The load neatly in place, he struck several matches in the process of getting the slicker pulled over every part of the saddle, so that the blood would not stain the leather.

He mounted then and rode off, leading Emory's horse at a very slow pace.

By the time he had ridden down the mesa on its far side and reached the outcrop of red sandstone, he had a reasonable recollection of this place. He left Emory's horse a few yards into the small badlands, dismounted himself and took his boots off.

Then he walked on ahead for perhaps a quarter of a mile, until he found the pinnacle rock which loomed blackly against the high stars. Now he was more careful, but just as sure. He made a thorough reconnoiter of the canyon wall for a hundred and fifty yards north, and found only one place where the talus under the wall would allow a man to climb its steep side. By a simple process of deduction, he knew this was the only place the cave would be, since it was the only place a man could climb up.

He climbed, a foot at a time, slowly, cautiously, with infinite patience. He was mildly gratified when he found the talus leveled off about forty feet up from the canyon floor, and he judged he was at the mouth of the cave.

Now he rose and moved almost carelessly, but slowly still, since he often stopped to listen. He did not think it strange that there was no thumping of his heart to fill the night with fear and sound. Presently he picked up the sound of rhythmical breathing. Moving toward it, he shifted his six-gun to his left hand, while he reached in his right pants pocket for matches. When he had them, he shifted the gun back to his right hand, took two matches in his left hand and reached above his head for the cave roof. It was low, barely clearing his head.

When the breathing was almost at his feet, he struck the matches on the roof. In their flare he saw Hand lying on his back on the cave floor.

Petrie cocked his gun and shot once, carefully, expertly, and then the light died. He struck two more, barely glancing at Hand, instead, searching the cave. He found a neat stack of wood along one wall, and he built up a roaring fire at the mouth of the cave, where Hand's fire had been.

And now he left Hand and went back to the horses and brought them both up to the foot of the talus. This next job had to be done carefully, so he worked slowly, sweating a little as he removed Emory from the saddle, cradled him in his arms and struggled up the slope with him. He had remembered to put on his boots again; but even with the aid of their digging heels, he had to rest twice before he reached the cave with his burden. Pausing to get his breath, he did not put Emory down until he searched out a likely place at the mouth of the cave. Then he laid him down there on his side, took Emory's gun, shot it twice at the sky, and wrapped the already stiffening fingers around the butt of it.

This done, he went over to Hand, raised him, dragged him two feet off his blanket and laid him on his face. Hand's gun he shot three times at the sky, then put carefully in Hand's hand.

All this was easy, he reflected, sweating from the exertion. Now he must be more careful. Taking a burning brand from the fire, he went down to Emory's horse. Removing the bloody slicker, he studied the saddle. Only the right stirrup had blood on it, and this he peeled off with his knife, rubbing dust on the place to darken it and make it look natural. Then, with the aid of the burning brand, he considered the ground. It was gravelly, so that tracks would not show. Satisfied, he took the slicker up to the cave, threw it on the fire, and prodded it until it had burned to ashes. He studied the footprints on the floor of the cave, and decided they would pass. Taking the blanket, he pulled it over Hand, placing the bloody spot over the red blot on Hand's back.

Lastly, he took another brand and went down the slope, this time caving in the prints of his stockinged feet and the deep prints of his heels. He mussed up the sand considerably, gouging it deeply as he came down.

Then he mounted, took the reins of Emory's horse and rode out the way he had come. Where he had first left the horses, he stopped and, without dismounting, lighted a match and leaned over in the saddle, studying the ground. It, too, was gravelly. There were several pebbles covered with blood where Emory's horse had stood. He leaned down and picked these up carefully and held them in his hand while he rode on.

When he reached grass, he threw the pebbles away, then made for the creek, although it was out of his way. Reaching it, he led his horse and Emory's through it several times. This was to wash off the blood on one hind fetlock of Emory's pony. Finished, he struck off in the direction of Clearcreek at a smart trot.

He reached it well after daylight, after pausing only once, and then only long enough to cache the two sacks of gold in a place where he could find them again.

In town, he rode straight to the sheriff's office. Honeywell was in, and Petrie greeted him curtly.

"I've just killed Hand and Emory," he announced pleasantly. "I thought you and Mayhew ought to know."

Honeywell's expression did not change when he heard the news. "Sit down," he said, indicating the other chair. Petrie sat down, and Sam said, "How'd it happen?"

Petrie went back to the finding of Breck's body, and his conviction that this war must stop. He told of going to Hartley, and Hartley taking him to the line camp. Emory, he said, offered to take him to Hand. They went to the red sandstone outcrop, up to the cave. Instead of hallooing, as any normal man would, Emory merely started up the talus to the cave. Petrie thought this was funny, but he supposed it was a prearranged way of coming in. At the mouth of the cave Emory spoke to Hand, who evidently was asleep. Hand grunted. Emory announced that Petrie was here to parley. Then all hell broke loose. Hand started shooting, and then Emory, panicked by his horse, started shooting, too, at Petrie. Petrie did the only thing he could. He shot once at Hand, then turned his fire on Emory, because he was closer and more dangerous. When it was over, he found he had killed Hand on the first lucky shot, and, of course, Emory too. It was self-defense. Hartley could testify to his good intentions, just as Nosey could. Hand's damned bullheadedness had got him and his foreman killed. Now what did Sam think of that?

Sam only said, "Well, that ends the war, don't it?"

"But not the way I wanted it to end," Petrie said glumly. "I had enough of this butchery, Sam. I didn't love Hand any the better for it; but at least I came to my senses. I was willing to make concessions, because

I had to." He spread his hands expressively, then let them fall. "Then this had to happen."

"It's tough," Sam said sadly, and for a moment Petrie wondered if Sam was mocking him.

"I did the best I could," Petrie said wearily. "If only Hand wasn't such a stubborn man."

Sam said nothing, only watched him.

"Well, here I am," Petrie said. "I don't know what you aim to do with me."

Sam said, "I can tell you better later." He rose with a grunt and hitched up his pants.

"Going to lock me up, Sam?" Petrie asked, without much interest.

"I reckon not. I know where to find you if I want you."

"I'll be around. I'll answer any questions you want me to."

"I know that," Sam said a little grimly. "You go get some sleep. I'll pick up Max, and we'll ride out and take a look."

"I didn't touch a thing," Petrie said. "I knew you'd want to see it."

"I reckon you did," Sam said dryly, stepping out the door.

Petrie watched him go, then rose and stood in the door. It was a beautiful morning, he noticed, clear, with a cool wind dusting the streets and making tiny dust devils in the road. The kind of a morning that gives a man an appetite, he thought, as he stepped out the door and headed for the café.

CHAPTER TWENTY

ON THE STREET, Flood paused before a darkened store front, knowing what he did next would carry a risk with it that he must minimize as much as possible. But balanced against that, and weighing stronger in his mind, was the safety of Margot. If all his plans must go overboard in making certain of that one thing, then they must go.

He knew it would be unsafe as well as unwise to let Klaus and these men think he had any connection with Margot. And yet he must get her and Teresa out of town, and safely. To do it, he must get her horse at the feed stable; but this would be the first place Klaus's men would watch. So be it. Let them watch.

It was still raining softly as he crossed the street and walked down to the stable. He paused in the wide door to wait for the night man, whose lantern he had seen moving in the office window.

When the man came out, Flood asked for his horse, tendering money to pay for it. He gave the man one coin, then held out another, saying, "Was there a woman, young, light-haired, who left a horse here tonight?"

"A sorrel, branded Wagon Hammer?"

"I wouldn't know," Flood said, giving him the coin. "If you are sure that is the horse, take him up to the hotel. She stopped me in the lobby and asked to have her horse brought up. She said you'd know."

The man, a stolid, slow-moving man of fifty or so, looked at the coin speculatively.

"When she want it?"

"She didn't say. She said to tie him out front."

"Don't she know it's rainin'?" the man asked quietly. "Even them saloon bums don't leave their ponies standing out in this."

"That's what she said," Flood replied. He started to walk down the centerway, then paused. "Isn't there some shelter back of the hotel you could put the horse under? Then leave word at the desk where you put him when you leave her change."

"I'll do that," the man said. "There's a shed back of the place."

Margot's horse was in the stall next to Flood's gray, and Flood loafed around saddling until the night man had finished with the sorrel and ridden out to deliver it. Then Flood rode out into the rain, and down the main street. His pace was slow, casual. And then, ahead in front of the marshal's office, he saw a half dozen men mount and ride south. He swung into the hitch-rack in front of the Bonanza, went in for a drink, and came out again soon. He reckoned these men had had time enough to clear out of town by now, and the stableman to deliver Margot's horse. It was as Teresa had predicted: Klaus and Brothers were taking care to guard the town and see she did not leave.

When he mounted again, he rode north, and when he came to a dark alley between two unlighted buildings he turned into it. It opened out on to the back lots of the buildings fronting the street, among which was the hotel. He found Margot's horse along with three others under a long, open-sided shed behind the hotel.

Satisfied, he set about his business. He rode north again now, keeping to the rear of the buildings until they thinned out and he was free of them and the town. He could not guess where Klaus's men would be on this side of town, so he swung over through the rock and brush to the road.

Once he looked back, and was pleased to see that the lights of Cienega were so dim that nothing could be seen in silhouette against them. Then he rode on, wary, waiting, his gray in an easy trot.

He was neither surprised nor unready, then, when, a little farther on, a voice called out of the night beside the trail, "Pull up, there!"

A match flared to light a lantern, but Flood was quick. He shot once, and the man holding the match dropped it. Then he spurred his gray, leaning down across his neck, and reined him off the road. Approaching the spot where the man who had the lantern was, he swerved his horse and crashed through the brush. Someone shot, cursing, and plunged through the brush, and then there were more shots, all wild, all guesses, all directed by the sound of his horse. And now he yanked his horse back to the road and continued up it, urging all the speed from his horse that he could get. A half mile on he paused and listened. He could hear nothing, but he knew they would come. Now he dismounted and carefully led his horse off the road, picking his slow and sodden way through the brush and boulders until the sound of horses approaching stopped him. He paused and stroked the neck of his horse, waiting.

He heard them approaching, an increasing calmness settling over him. His horse was blowing, but that would be lost in the racket they made. And through the rain, riding on it, it seemed, they drew even with him in a splashing, sucking, slogging wave, which held a moment and then died into slow-fading silence and gave way to the insistent murmur of the rain. Three of them, he guessed.

He rode back to town, through the back lots to the shed at the rear of the hotel. Walking through the long corridor, he sat down in the lobby, where he could see the street. He could only guess at the time he would have to wait if he had been successful. But this time came and passed, but still he sat, wondering. Then, as he was about to abandon his chair, a half dozen horsemen rode up from the south and pulled up at the marshal's office. They had a few words with a man from the office, whom Flood could not see, then they rode on, north.

Flood waited a few moments, then went upstairs, nodding pleasantly to the desk man.

Margot and Teresa were dressed and waiting. While Flood was gone, Margot had stepped out and bought a slicker for Teresa. They looked at him expectantly, and he said, "Let's try it."

He told them to give him two minutes, then to go down the back way to the shed at the rear of the building.

Margot said, "Will it work, Mark?"

"If you can find your way up the mountain in this rain, it will." And he smiled, wondering if she suspected how little he knew if it would succeed or fail.

He left them then and went down the back stairs himself. Out in the rain again, he knew he must find a horse for Margot, and he knew where he would go. To buy one would leave a trail for Klaus to follow. Then he must take one. Across these back lots in the rear of the assay office, he had seen a saddled horse in a shed. He went back to it now. The horse was dry, the saddle and bridle blankets thrown over the manger.

Flood lighted a match and considered the horse, a tough, stocky roan with a deep chest and short legs. The saddle he only glanced at. It was old and worn. Then he saddled up the roan, left enough money on the manger to pay for the horse and saddle, and led it out and back to the hotel.

Teresa and Margot were waiting. They mounted and rode off, Flood in the lead. He still clung to the back lots, but this time he rode south. At this edge of the town they were forced to the road by the deep jut of rock that narrowed the canyon at this place until only the road and the river could knife by it. This was where they would meet trouble, and Flood ordered them to stop while he rode ahead.

But he went unchallenged past the rock. And only now did he realize that he had played in luck, and that the thin and tenuous probability of these men believing his ruse had been stronger than he had reckoned.

The three of them passed the rock and, once past, hurried. The rain held on, and the night was black and thick, so that Flood knew the finding of the trail up the mountainside would take long and weary search. He tried to recall all the landmarks near the place where the trail joined the road, and he could, but they were useless if they could not be seen. He did remember a greasy, musky pothole in the road that was less than a minute's ride from the trail. He found it now, filled with a foot of water. And from there he found the trail with no trouble at all.

Turning up it, he let his gray have the rein, and he found that the horse followed the trail without any difficulty.

Satisfied, he stopped and dismounted while Teresa and Margot pulled up beside him in the dripping trees.

"Good luck," he said quietly. "Ride hard and long,

and follow me into Clearcreek from the Silver Creek range."

"Mark," Margot said quietly. "What if your trail won't take you to Clearcreek?"

"It will."

She dismounted now and came over to him. "You'll be careful, Mark?" she asked gently. "I only understand enough of this to guess how it will end. He will fight, you know."

She could almost see the quiet smile on his face. It was the first time she had referred to this man he was hunting, and even now she did not know why she had said this. She only knew she had put into words what she had been thinking, guessing, and now she asked, "Do you know who he will be, Mark?"

"I think I knew long ago," he told her quietly. "I had to get proof."

"You won't tell me?"

"No. I have to be fair."

Margot put her arms around him and kissed him. Because she needed the power his body and his nearness could give her. But since the first time he had kissed her and told her that there were things that must be finished before he could come to her, she had felt him hold himself back when she was in his arms. It was something within him, she knew, that would not allow him to give himself until he could give wholly. And she loved him more for it even as his body stiffened and his lips were cold and ungenerous.

"Teresa depends on you," Flood said gently, and Margot smiled secretly at the gentle evasion, the reminder that she must wait. She wondered if he never needed the strength only someone who loved him could give.

And, as if reading her mind, Flood said quietly, "All you are thinking now I will answer, Margot."

"I had no right to do that," she said. "But I can play this game, Mark."

"All the way through?" Flood asked.

"All the way."

Flood did not speak for a moment, then he said, simply, "Good-by."

He went over to Teresa as Margot mounted. "It's all over now, except the drudgery."

"I nearly killed you tonight," Teresa said curiously. "Why are women so blind?"

Flood thought of her face, beautiful and lovely, but so hardened and cynical that she never let a man see her real self.

"Why are men?" he asked.

Flood stepped back and they rode off. Walking over to his horse, he wondered if his luck would hold. But at the hotel, after inquiring if anybody had been to see him, and being told they had not, he believed it had. He went to his room, undressed and was immediately asleep.

He was wakened before daylight by Klaus hammering on his door. He lighted the lamp and let him in. Klaus was wet and surly, and he did not bother to introduce the man with him, a middle-aged man with a square face and narrow eyes, who stepped into the room but did not sit down as Klaus did. Flood dressed quickly.

"How much did you tell this girl?" Klaus demanded.

"Teresa? About our proposition? Nothing. Why?"

"She's gone," Klaus said savagely, drumming the table with his fingers.

"You damned fool," Flood said quietly. "How much did she know?"

"If you didn't tell her, I don't reckon she knew much. At any rate, no more than she knew already, and that wouldn't bother us here much. She don't know the time nor the place."

"Then you're going to take me to see your man?" Flood asked.

"Why do you think I come up here?" Klaus demanded.

"To admit you were bullheaded, I hope," Flood said quietly. "Where do we go?"

Klaus regarded him hostilely, as if he wished to hold

the secret as long as he could. "Clearcreek," he said curtly.

Flood raised his eyebrows in feigned surprise and said, "Who is it over there?"

"You'll find that out," Klaus said.

It was on Flood's tongue to argue him into reasonableness, but he refrained. If he forced the issue they might become suspicious. He shrugged instead and said, "I haven't eaten since yesterday afternoon. Can you spare the time?"

"I thought you were in such a hell of a hurry you were leaving this morning," Klaus said bluntly.

"I was in a hurry to make your minds up for you," Flood replied. "I'm eating. Come along if you want."

Klaus's companion looked questioningly at his boss, but Klaus got up and said, "All right."

There was not yet false dawn in the east when the three of them crossed to the café. Flood wanted to delay their start as long as possible, so as to let the rain wash out the tracks Margot and Teresa would leave, for the rain was still slanting down in a raw, everlasting drizzle. By the time they had finished eating it was beginning to lighten in the east.

Flood started across to the hotel when Klaus said, "Now where?"

"My horse is behind the hotel," Flood said.

"What's he doing there?" Klaus demanded. "I saw him in the stable last night."

"I brought him over," Flood said. "I reckoned you would be ready to leave around midnight." He looked Klaus over insolently. "You look like you needed cash worse than you do."

Klaus let the jab ride, and he and his companion went down to the stable while Flood settled his hotel score and got his horse. Riding around to the feed stable, he was careful to rein his horse through all the mud and water he could find, so that by the time he arrived there, fresh mud was plastered on his gray's legs and belly.

At the stable, Klaus was waiting beside his horse in

conversation with his companion, to whom he was evidently giving orders.

When Flood rode up beside him, Klaus gathered his reins up and said, "Well, if you aim to stick to that thousand head cut, Flood, I'm wasting my time. But I'll go."

"I don't think you are," Flood said.

Klaus shrugged. "This man doesn't argue. He just tells you."

"Sure," Flood said.

Klaus squinted up at him in the rain. "Once in a while you see a proud man that's never been licked. He rides like you, Flood, and he talks like you, and he even looks like you. But once in his life he meets a man that he tries to cut his dogs loose on, and this man won't take it." He turned to his companion, who was grinning, and said to him, "You ought to be along."

Flood said slowly, "Once in a while you ride up beside a man that you'd like to kick in the mouth. You'd like to kick all his teeth down his throat. I haven't got much patience."

He loosed a foot in the stirrup and Klaus stepped back, his hand falling to his gun. Flood only laughed and wheeled his horse and rode out into the street.

Klaus soon caught up with him and said grimly, "This is going to make you sweat, Flood, that's all."

CHAPTER TWENTY-ONE

THEY RODE HARD THAT FIRST DAY in a driving, relentless rain that piled down the canyons on gusty, whipping wings. They could not have talked if they wanted to, and they did not. Part of the time they were in a boiling fury of clouds that swept past them in writhing tendrils of fog, so that the trail and all the visible landmarks were obscured. Flood wondered if Margot would lose her way in it, and he cursed himself for not having provided food for her in case she was forced to wander days among these peaks before she found her way out. But he put this out of his mind as soon as he thought of it. He tested himself, and saw that he remembered every turn and twist, every canyon, every switchback of the tortuous trail. If he could remember it, then she could, too. The thought comforted him somewhat.

They did not stop at noon. The rain had eased off a little, but the wind held, driving the drizzle before it that turned to sleet later. Klaus had evidently understood Flood, for he made no talk.

His slack, heavy body sat the saddle like a rock, and he seemed intent on holding the pace he had set—a steady, mile-eating one that counted no time out for blowing the horses or pulling in the lee of a rock to dismount and stamp chilled blood into circulation again.

Flood was surprised when, just at dark, Klaus left the trail for a side canyon. Half way up to it he dismounted before a cave in the canyon wall under whose overhang of rock there was room for both horses and men. There was wood stacked neatly against one wall and a tow sack of grain which swung out from a crack in the wall by a wire to keep it from mice. Klaus built a fire while Flood grained the horses and rubbed them down. Soon, both men were drying out their clothes and warming up for the first time since they left. The comfort of it seemed to thaw out Klaus, and his eyes were a little less hostile as he watched Flood.

Flood decided to see if he would talk, and he said casually, "Ever try a drive in this weather?"

"Drive?" Klaus said blankly.

"I saw several signs," Flood said carelessly. "There have been cattle through here. I thought maybe they were your outfits."

Klaus did not answer for a moment, then, as if he had resigned himself to Flood sharing the knowledge of all this with him, said, "It's purely hell. We had to hold a herd back yonder one night in a snow that all but bogged us in."

Flood chuckled appreciatively, but said nothing.

"We started them off before daylight. We figured if we waited another hour we'd be there forever. We come through all right."

"You've just got to take a chance, then?" Flood said easily.

"That's it. Last time we got the herd in a rain, drove them in a rain, walked into this snow here and delivered them in a rain. We earned that money," Klaus said, shaking his head with the memory of the misery of that trip. He sighed. "But that's the weather we need."

That would have been Shifflin's herd, Flood thought calmly. He wanted to ask a thousand questions now, but he did not dare. As long as Klaus talked willingly it was all right. But to ask questions would be dangerous.

But Klaus was sleepy and showed no disposition to talk, so Flood had to be content. He had more proof now, besides what Klaus had dropped, that these men had taken the Shifflin herd. Klaus yawned, got his blankets and announced he was turning in. Flood followed him, and was soon asleep. Just before he sank into sleep, he thought of Margot and Teresa, who were probably huddled together in the shelter of some rocks far up the trail, waiting for daylight. And when he thought of Margot, he thought of what tomorrow would bring for him, and he welcomed it because of her. Tomorrow he would be a dead man or a free man. So he slept, content.

The day broke clear, with a cold, frosty wind that had a bite to it. They hit the trail early, hungry, but not so cold now that they were in the saddle. The sleet and snow had been washed away by a later rain.

By noon they were sloping down through the notch on to the Silver Creek range, and the day was warm, almost hot under a clear sky. Flood had withdrawn into himself, for all there was to do now was wait. He could find no signs on the Silver Creek range that riders had preceded them, but he laid that to Margot's wisdom in covering her trail.

The ride to Clearcreek seemed endless. Klaus was almost garrulous this morning, but nothing he said seemed to affect Flood. When they topped the hill into Clearcreek, Flood's face was composed, yet alert. For a moment he wondered if he had been wrong, if Klaus was hunting some other man, but he asked no questions. It was as if all this was out of his hands now, and would unfold and conclude without him and in spite of him, as if all he had done at the start to set it in motion had vanished in this hour.

They rode down the street, past riders and wagons and people that seemed one with the sunny indolence of the afternoon, to pull in at the hitch-rack to one side of the Palace. Flood looked across to the sheriff's office, and saw Honeywell standing in the door, regarding him with impassive curiosity. Flood only shook his head and Honeywell nodded, did not move.

"Will he be here?" Flood asked, as he dismounted beside Klaus.

"I reckon. I'll find out."

Flood said, "It wouldn't be wise for me to go in, would it?"

Klaus looked at him thoughtfully.

"I mean my name and all. If he lives here, the two of us ought not to be connected. Remember, I had a brother here."

"You're right," Klaus said, nodding.

"I wouldn't even mention the name," Flood said. "Not in there. When we're alone it will be all right."

"Sure," Klaus said. He swung under the hitch-rack.

Flood turned and walked across the street to the sheriff's office. As he walked, he took out his six-gun and rammed the shells out into the dust of the street and put fresh loads in. When he was finished, he was fronting the hitch-rack before the sheriff's office. Sam was still standing there.

"Did you notice him, Sam?" Flood asked.

Sam nodded.

"Go over and see who he talks to. Don't arrest him now; but don't let him go, either. He's a man you want."

Sam stepped nimbly out of the door, swung under

the hitch-rack and said to Flood as he passed, "Trouble?"

"The end of it, I think," Flood said.

Then he turned and leaned on the hitch-rack. He looked down the street once to make sure nobody would be crossing when he shouldn't, and then he looked up it. He saw Margot and Teresa were riding down it now. They approached, and Teresa swung into the hitch-rack by Flood's horse.

Margot reined her horse in the middle of the street and looked at Flood.

"In there?" she asked, her low voice carrying plainly across the distance.

"I think so," Flood said.

"Mark," Margot said, although Flood was watching her. She looked at him a moment, then said, "Square my end of it, too, Mark. I'm Margot Munro, you see. That's what I never told you."

Flood understood this, understood it while looking at the dark door of the Palace knifed by the bat-wing doors. He understood that she had ridden into the hitch-rack, and that the sun was warm on his shoulders, and that the quiet somnolence of this afternoon was gathering to burst.

When he saw the legs under the bat-wing doors, then saw them break open, he straightened up and started to walk slowly across the road, and he said, "Ah," quietly, with deep and welcome satisfaction.

Petrie came out first, Klaus behind him, Honeywell behind him.

Then Petrie stopped dead. He had seen Flood.

Flood came on to the middle of the street and paused, his hands loose at his sides.

"This is it, Petrie," he said, and his voice ripped across the still afternoon like a whip.

There is a haste which is harnessed panic, and it was this that stirred through Petrie like a chilling wind as he clawed down for his gun and brought it out and shot and hit the hitch-rack in front of him, and shot again and crashed a window behind Flood, while Flood raised his gun in a visible, deliberate arc bisected by the click of the gun-cock, raised it eye-high for the certain sight he needed and let the hammer go.

Petrie's third shot boomed against the high false front of the sheriff's office, and then he brought his gun hand, with its gun, and his other hand to his chest even while he was falling, so that he fell on crossed clawing hands. He shuddered that way, his head lowered a little over the edge of the board sidewalk as if he were a child looking for a coin that had slipped through and under the walk.

Flood's gaze shuttled past Honeywell with his gun in Klaus's back and settled on Margot, who sat her horse as still as stone. Flood nodded once and she raised a hand off her leg in that loose, friendly gesture of salute.

Flood said to Honeywell, "Is the Wagon Hammer inside?"

"Max will take care of that."

"Not all of it," Flood said. He came up on the walk and said, "Bring that man in here."

Inside, eight or ten Wagon Hammer riders were at the bar. They were all looking at Mayhew, who leaned against the front wall, his gun covering them. Flood saw their faces change as they looked at him.

He began, "Have any of you ever heard of the Munro herd that was rustled down by the Point Loma breaks last year some time?"

"You hangin' that on us, too?" one of the Wagon Hammer hands asked bluntly.

"Have you?" Flood insisted.

Several men nodded, and Flood went on, "Last week, three thousand head of cattle from Texas under nine men and a trail boss named Shifflin disappeared one night from a bedground on the Ruidoso. The men were killed, the cattle were driven across your range, into the notch at the head of Silver Creek range and sold in Cienega, across the mountains. Do any of you know who planned the steal?"

This time they said nothing.

"Petrie did," Flood said quietly. "He brought a gang

over from Cienega for both jobs." He indicated Klaus.
"This man will back me up."

Klaus said huskily, "You got the wrong man, mister."

Flood turned to Sam. "He went to Petrie?"

"Ask Max," Honeywell said. "He was at the bar."

Mayhew said, "He came up to Loosh and said, 'A
gent wants to see you outside.' Petrie finished his drink
and went out."

"Want to talk now?" Flood said to Klaus.

This time Klaus nodded. He looked at the Wagon
Hammer men and said, "That's right. All he said."

Flood said to them, "You weren't fighting for range
when you fought for Petrie. You were fighting for that
notch that led into the trail over the mountains to
Cienega. Petrie had to have that for an outlet for his
trail rustling. Hand moved in on Silver Creek, and
Petrie had to fight for it or quit. He fought." He paused,
regarding them soberly. "If you don't want to crowd
your luck, ride out of here. No man has said the Wagon
Hammer hands were in on these steals. Hand wins this
war, and you men have cleaner hands than his Bar
Stirrup. I'd get out."

The men looked stubbornly from Flood to Mayhew.
Honeywell said, "If it's Breck you are wondering about,
I killed him. I don't know just why I killed him, but I
reckon I'll find out soon." He added dryly, "I didn't
think anybody connected with the Wagon Hammer
would mourn him."

One of the Wagon Hammer hands laid a gun gently
on the counter and stepped out. "I've wanted to do this
for a long time. There's my ticket," he said cheerfully.

He walked past Flood and out the door, paused to
gaze down at Petrie, then they could hear him whistle
softly as he walked down the street.

Honeywell touched Flood's arm and gave him his
gun. "Hold this on your friend a minute. This is all
over, I reckon."

He stepped outside to Petrie, then leaned over and
with much effort pulled off Petrie's boots. He examined
the sock feet of the dead man and then came into the

saloon again. Walking up to the bar, he reached a fat hand in his shirt pocket and brought out a small buckle, which he laid on the bar.

He said to the Wagon Hammer men, "Loosh killed Emory and Hand. I wondered why a man would be padding around in his sock feet out there, and I figured it about the same as you would. Emory bled quite a bit. Loosh stepped in it when he went back to his horse after killing Hand. What got me to wonderin' was that there was a bullet hole in Hand's blanket. I dug the slug out of the dirt floor." He indicated the buckle. "That was off Emory's bloody slicker he burned. You men still want to fight for him?"

Flood looked across at Mayhew. "Ben Hand is dead, then?"

Mayhew nodded. "There are people here who wouldn't have let him live anyway. Maybe it's best."

And now Flood turned to Klaus. "There were ten men with that last herd Petrie stole. Where are they?"

Klaus licked his lips and seemed unable to speak.

"Dead?" Flood asked.

Klaus nodded once. "We caved a cutbank over them out there in that shale beyond the Barrier Rim."

Suddenly this room and its men had become unbearable to Flood, and he turned and left, and it was like walking out of a life. It was over, he thought wearily, with no man the victor, and dead in the ashes of their own burning.

He started toward the hotel, noticing that Margot and Teresa were not at the hitch-rack, and he did not wonder at it, for he was thinking that a woman who had the patience to wait as long as Margot had waited would have the patience to see it through—all through.

When Honeywell dropped in beside him, Flood knew he was going to the hotel, too.

"To see why I killed Breckenridge," Honeywell explained, his sad face a little fretted—nothing else.

The door to Margot's room was open and she was sitting on the bed. She rose at sight of them, and Honeywell removed his hat.

"That morning you left, I killed Breckenridge," he said quietly. "Mind telling me why he was following you?"

"I am Margot Munro, Sam," Margot said simply. "I came here after Dad died. The theft of his herd ruined him, and he died two months later. Lee and I came here, hoping we could find the persons who stole the herd." She shrugged wearily. "You know about Loosh and myself. I don't know the rest, except this." She looked at Flood briefly. "When I loved Mark, Petrie knew. I think he believed I had sent for Mark, because Mark saved his life and did not kill him. He fought him and did not kill him. Loosh saw and understood. The night I went to warn Mark at Hartley's cabin, Loosh or Breck or both searched my room. I think they were after the letters they were sure Mark had written me. They came across these."

She indicated a sheaf of letters on the table. "I was unwise enough to save them—letters from my mother addressed to Margot Munro that I saved all these years since she died. When they saw the name, they knew they must get rid of us. They killed Lee, and—and—"

"Breck was after you," Honeywell said. He turned, the fretted lines gone from his face, mumbling his thanks, and then at the door he paused. He looked long at Flood and then at Margot.

"Will you forget all the trouble it took to bring you together?" he asked gently of them both. And then he added gravely, smiling a little, "If it didn't sound to bad to say it, I would say out loud that it was worth it. You are a fine sight. A fine sight."

He closed the door gently behind him. Margot came over to Flood's arms and leaned her forehead against his shoulder. Then she looked up at him.

"Shall we finish it all, Mark—all this that stands between us yet?"

Flood said, "Is there any more?"

"Teresa. Could we leave her here to run our hotel?" And when Flood began to smile, she said, "I promised to see it clear through—all of it. Remember?"

Flood nodded, smiling broadly now.

"She could run it while we are away. Are we going away?"

"If you say. Where?"

"Home, your home, our home. Is it all finished now, Mark?" she asked quietly.

But he found that he did not have to say yes, and she discovered that she did not need an answer.